WARNING

This book contains sexually explicit scenes and adult language. It may be considered offensive to some readers. This book is for sale to adults ONLY.

* * * * * * * * * * * * * * * * * *

Please store your files wisely where they cannot be accessed by underage readers.

This story is Book One of "The Bill Griffin Space Adventure Series"

Book 1 – Blue Balzar: Exploding

Bill Griffin thought he was on his way to realize his dreams among the stars, toward the love of his life, Clarity. Then his world just blows up before his eyes. Literally. An unlikely crew of beautiful, exotic, female aliens finds and takes Bill aboard their spaceship. As he reluctantly tags along on a quest for galactic excitement and dangerous adventure, he develops an unlikely camaraderie among the women on board.

Blue Balzar: Exploding

The Bill Griffin Space Adventure Series

Book 1

By W.D. Banecroft

Table of Contents

Chapter 1: The Worst Day Ever

"**WELL, SHIT**," said Bill Griffin. It was a thoroughly appropriate thing for him to say, if a bit understated. Because, as an astronaut on assignment on the moon, he had one of the best views in existence of the Earth as it erupted into a fiery hell.

It happened pretty quickly, like what-in-hell-just-happened speed. One moment, Bill had been out on a day-mission driving the moon buggy to check on the base's outermost communication marker, not thinking about much at all apart from doing his job and just admiring the big blue ball in the sky. The next moment, that same blue ball sprouted a giant green bubble out of North America. That bubble grew and burst into a mess of fiery green that blew all the clouds away.

At the same time, other green pimples appeared at irregular intervals over the planet. The pattern was the same as the first, and in moments dear old Earth was engulfed entirely as if the Hulk had swallowed it.

"What the fuck," Bill said, but it wasn't a question. He wasn't petrified with fear or panic just yet. What he was seeing didn't seem real enough for that. He just stopped the moon buggy and stared up into the sky in confusion, not really believing his eyes.

Belatedly, he thought to turn on his communicator, and right away wished that he hadn't. A booming babble of voices crashed and jabbered through the speaker in his helmet and he did what he could to lower the volume, yet the screaming was alarming.

He might as well not have bothered. He could make no sense of the fearful questions and horror-filled expletives. The only thing that came through clearly was emotional terror, and that he, Bill Griffin, wasn't imagining anything. The other astronauts at the moon base were panicked and dismayed, stunned and shocked. It was an orgy of fear and horror at the transition from home to hell.

He managed to pick out a few salient snippets from the overwhelming ocean of fright. "… Alien ships… energy weapons of some sort… appeared out of nowhere… oh God, oh God… no!" Like that, only mostly buried in a hubbub that sounded like the zoo's monkey enclosure at mealtime.

Nor did it end with the Earth simply burning in bright, putrid green. As he sat in the driver's seat in the moon buggy and the sweat of true terror beaded on the inside of his helmet, Bill thought he could see lines of energy where the alien ships continued to fire. The Earth couldn't take it. It collapsed in on itself, and then, seconds later, silently exploded outward as if it were trying to imitate a supernova.

"Shit," Bill said again as the great flaming mass erupted toward him. In seconds, what had once been Bill's favorite planet had blossomed to twice, thrice, four times its original size, and it kept growing. "Shit, shit, shit!" Bill yelled, unconsciously adding his own voice to the babble of noise streaming through his communication equipment.

Panic engulfed him, but there was little he or anyone could do. The explosion from Earth was growing bigger and bigger, and Bill knew without any doubt that it would soon engulf the moon. Destroying him and the others when it did.

Bill had to act, had to do something. In mindless terror, afraid for his very life and heedless of the reality that without a home planet to return to, he did the only thing he could think of and threw himself from the moon buggy. His life was effectively over anyway; he'd be damned if his last moments wouldn't be filled with some outward sign of bravery.

He raised his middle finger at the growing green menace, picked up a moon rock, and threw it at the devastating explosive mass. "Fuck you!" screamed Bill as he watched the moon rock take a seemingly slow-motion low-gravity flight with no chance of landing before the moon would be destroyed.

With the same aching slowness of movement at one-sixth the gravitational pull of Earth, Bill willed himself to touch the moon surface with knees and palms, even if one palm was part of his prosthetic hand. As soon as he did, he ducked down beside the moon buggy and desperately burrowed under the sand, as if that could save him.

"Shit. Fuck. Piss," he said, even though he rarely swore. The situation seemed to call for something a little more extreme than his usual vocabulary. Still full of anger, he punched the moon buggy with his left hand, the prosthetic. Usually hardy, his fist got caught on an unyielding bit of machinery, and two of Bill's fake fingers detached. "Well, isn't this just the greatest fucking end to a great fucking day?"

The attached hand and forearm were a step up from what he had before he joined the service. As part of the Lunar Maintenance Service benefits, the upgraded prosthetic was provided to ensure he could perform his duties properly. He'd only had it since basic training. But now, it was wrecked.

As Bill watched his fingers float away, the last thing he heard before the leading wave of the explosion reached the part of the moon that he had called home for the past few weeks was a desperate wail over the speakers in his helmet. "No! The ships—one of them is heading this way!"

Chapter 2: All By Myself

Bill's space suit was a remarkable feat of engineering. It was designed to keep him alive in the most inimical conditions imaginable. Within its snug confines, he could withstand the icy cold of space without even a smidge of frostbite. The helmet's visor protected his eyes against the sun's radiation, and the oxygen tank on his back allowed him to breathe freely for a full workday. He could even move about with relative ease.

But what the designers of the suit had never foreseen was that on the day the Earth was blown up by an unknown number of enemy spaceships, Bill's left side would be totally exposed to the fire and fury of the Earth's demise for a full thirty-two seconds and change.

In addition, he was hit by a multitude of mostly tiny pieces of rock that had once been part of Earth's core, the bedrock beneath the Atlantic Ocean, and the stone border around old Mrs. Beadle's prized peony garden.

Nevertheless, Bill's quick thinking saved him from the worst of it. Had he stayed in the driver's seat of the moon buggy, he would have been no more than a smear of strawberry jam beneath a boulder that might once have been under the North Pole. Ho ho ho.

Astonishingly, his suit kept him alive, the self-repairing nano-molecules having recovered somewhat from the temporary onslaught. His left side was singed and some of his head-up displays were fritzing out, and his CO2 scrubber had been damaged. But when the first howl of fire and brimstone passed, Bill was still able to haul himself up to a sitting position. At least his suit wasn't leaking air.

He looked in confusion first at the squashed moon buggy and then the still-burning heavens where the Earth had been, blinked dazedly in his helmet, and said, quite clearly, "Fuck me."

With the magnitude of his situation sinking in, he tapped his helmet. "Hello? Is anyone… is anyone still alive?" He heard his voice choke up, but figured he'd earned it. He'd just watched the only world he'd ever known blow up in his face. The moon was now the biggest object between Venus and Mars, and Bill assumed the whole solar system would be shuddering as a result. He certainly was.

The only reply he received was static. Bill tried again. "Hello? Is anyone fucking there?" he asked hesitantly. Even to his own ears, he sounded small and sad, like a child lost in the woods, desperate for human contact. He was starting to get it now, starting to realize he only had a few hours to live. Maybe he would have a bit longer if he could make it back to the base, but with the buggy smashed under the boulder, there was little hope of going anywhere.

Unless someone from the base was able to rescue him?

It wasn't much of a hope, but Bill was desperate. He was willing to grasp at the thinnest of straws and trust his whole weight to it in a heartbeat. At this stage of panic, he would have sold one of his kidneys and half a lung just to hear another human voice. Hell, he would have sold *both* kidneys. What was the difference between dying of uremia and dying of starvation or oxygen deprivation? The only difference was the timing, but in the end, death would ultimately reign.

The base was equipped for no more than a few months, a year and a half at most, if one were to seriously ration. Beyond that, well, there would be no more supply ships from Earth.

"Hello?" The anxiety in his voice was plain to hear. Had Earth's explosion knocked out his comms? Or had it ruined the base beyond all hope of anyone surviving?

He tapped his helmet again, and for a moment the static cleared. "… Oh God!" was all he heard, and the crackle returned.

Nevertheless, that simple exclamation buoyed him immensely. Someone else was still alive! Bill wasn't the last fucking living thing on Ear—on the moon!

He was so excited that he almost cried out in pure joy. He clambered to his feet and looked back toward the base. Bill knew he was a long way from the others, but he might just be able to make out part of the main dome if he was lucky.

He wasn't lucky. In fact, he was decidedly unlucky. Just as he'd been in about the best position in the universe to view Earth's destruction, he was also in the best position ever to witness the deaths of every other human on the moon.

Bill could indeed see just the very top of the main dome. It was far away, but not too far that the moon's curvature obscured it completely.

Unfortunately, he could also see the dark, alien spacecraft reflected in the sun, directly above that dome.

It was a thing of nightmares, made of malignance and terror, and completely lacking in elegance. It looked like someone had gathered a random collection of plate iron and welded it into an uncomfortable shape. It looked like an expression of pain, and it hurt Bill to look at it.

Then it hurt even more. A single green pulse burst from the spacecraft to the base, and that was that. An explosion, just like Bill had seen erupting from Earth, but on a far smaller scale, yet the same blazing green.

It was a silent detonation, like those of Earth, he guessed. The moon shook beneath his feet, and the shock wave knocked him roughly over the rocks. But it was beyond catastrophic. Bill's comms had clicked in again just at the wrong moment. His head was filled with the screams of people he'd known and worked with, some of whom he'd called friends. He screamed with them.

There was no doubt in his mind. They were all dead in an instant as their cries abruptly ceased. Bill's sympathy scream died in a choking sob.

He was truly, completely alone, as nobody had ever been alone before. He turned back to what was left of Earth while helplessness kicked his stomach and loneliness bit his heart.

"Fuck a duck. Sideways," he muttered. "Fuck it twice."

Chapter 3: All I Need is the Air

The continuing show put on by the still dying Earth was nothing if not spectacular. Bill sat on the front end of the squashed moon buggy with his back against the boulder that had tried to kill him and kicked his feet rhythmically in the air as he watched. After the wave of fire and rock had passed, the sky remained lit by a hundred million oversized sparklers that had once formed his home, all radiating out from where Earth had once been.

It was like the largest firework ever imagined had exploded, littering the sky with its afterimage and frozen in time.

And yet, not frozen at all. Just slowed down, so Bill could watch the progress of each glowing piece of rock, now part of a new asteroid cloud.

He remembered a time when he was young, alone, and lying down on the hill at the back of his aunt's house, staring at the sky. He'd stayed there for ages, unmindful of the dew on the grass that soaked into his shirt and made him shiver. On that day, the sky had been clear of clouds and smog, and the stars had seemed close enough to touch if one would just reach up.

The sky had been so clear that Bill had been able to see a number of satellites tracing their paths across the heavens.

For him, a boy with few real friends, it had been a magical night. Perhaps it had even contributed to his decision to follow his all-time, all-encompassing high-school crush, Clarity Thomas, to the stars.

Either way, the Earth's death provided a view a hundred-thousand times more spectacular, and infinitely sadder. As each fiery remnant snuffed itself out in the cold of space, Bill couldn't help but think of everyone he knew who were no longer.

His aunt. Her on-again, off-again boyfriend. The people he'd grown up with even if they never knew each other that well. His teachers. The other recruits who went through training at the same time as he did, many of whom had made it off-world only to die on the moon. Even the faceless voices on the other side of the games he'd played, like Lord Roosevelt, Rex Krotos, and Bonny Bu.

Beyond them, Bill felt more connected with the hundreds of actors and actresses who'd helped him while away his time when he was most lonely. They were gone, too, as were the countless strangers he'd bumped into once or twice, never knowing who they were.

Gone. All gone, in just a few minutes. One moment they had been going about their normal lives, and the next they'd been consumed by the angry green holocaust spat in their direction by malevolent aliens.

It was like the plot of a bad science fiction story, but not a long one. The bad guys had already won, and as for the hero… well, there was only Bill left, and just at that moment, all alone on the moon with his oxygen running out, he didn't feel very fucking heroic.

He felt sad more than anything else. Sad that he'd never see the new superhero movie that came out on the same day he'd gone into space. Sad that he would never taste another meat lover's pizza with the BBQ sauce he loved. Sad that he would never see another dawn from his aunt's front window, or any window for that matter. Or any dawn.

And, if he was honest, he was sad that he would never have sex again, even if sex had never been a big part of his life. But in his grieving mind, it was just as valid a thing to miss as anything else. Bill was painfully aware that his sex life existed only in his fantasy. Completely one-sided. Or should he say, one-handed. But never to have sex with a real-life, flesh and blood woman went against all laws of nature, didn't it?

And pikelets! Pikelets were his favorite food ever, and he would never taste their fluffy, lighter-than-air, golden goodness again. He would never bite into their softness and feel the heavenly warm flesh smothered in butter and hot syrup.

Truth be told, he would have settled for plain old American pancakes or waffles as a last meal. After visiting an international food festival and tasting pikelets for the first time, he was a convert for life. Pikelets tasted how he imagined sex to feel. They were just that perfect.

Bill had used up his quota of swearwords for one day. Likely, for his entire life. Instead, he whispered, "Pikelets," into his helmet in the same way he might have whispered the name of a lover, if he happened to have one. He sighed, ignoring the very unmanly tears that were leaking from his eyes, and absently started to hum.

He didn't choose the song, exactly. Rather it was supplied to him by his subconscious. Nevertheless, it was remarkably apt. A song originally sung by an icon of Earth before Bill was born, featuring a certain Major Tom who was lost all alone in space.

It was a sad song, and it suited his melancholy frame of mind perfectly.

About halfway through, a warning beeped from his wrist console. A single glance told him all he needed to know.

Low oxygen. Cartridge change required.

Surprisingly, Bill managed a laugh. "Thanks for the fucking warning," he said. The irony was complete. He would have loved to return to base, if the base still existed. He would have been overjoyed if only to replace his oxygen tank with a fresh one.

But he was alone on an empty planet, or satellite, actually, and he imagined the base was no more than a charred spot glowing beyond the horizon. There were no oxygen cartridges available. No pockets of air for him to breathe.

Nothing. Not a fucking damn thing left.

He could very well be the last human being alive, and all he could do was sit and wait for his air to run out.

Maybe one day, some sentient creature would wander by and find his corpse still sitting on the front bracket of his crumpled moon buggy and wonder what his story was. Wonder how he had lost some fingers. Or maybe he would sit there for all eternity, undisturbed. Bravo, Griffin. Good to see you are living up to your potential, you loser extraordinaire.

As the warning beeper started to get really excited because he wasn't paying it the attention it demanded, Bill suddenly thought that maybe he *wasn't* the last human being alive. The lack of oxygen in his blood must have been starving his brain. The alien ship had been careful to destroy the moon base, but there were other pockets of humanity dotted throughout the solar system.

There was the International Space Station, a permanently occupied home for more than two hundred people. There was the Mars colony, which was almost self-sufficient. Maybe the alien scum who'd blown up the Earth had overlooked it. Maybe humanity had some sort of chance.

And then, Bill realized as his beeper finally decided he was past helping, there was also the new base in the asteroid belt.

As he yawned in his helmet and wondered if he should rest his eyes for a bit, he thought that perhaps Clarity Thomas, the girl, or now woman, of his dreams, might still be alive, might still have a passing thought of him, of his potential.

He hoped that she was. Maybe she could somehow make her way to the Mars colony, if it still existed.

Bill hoped she would make it. One day, somehow, he thought they might end up together.

It was a pleasant thought, and he rested his helmet against the crumpled aluminum at his back. The light show had largely faded to black, and he felt surprisingly peaceful, even though the rate of his breathing quickened due to the low oxygen level. With an image of Clarity Thomas looming large in his memory, he thought that maybe he could nap just for a moment.

But it wasn't to be. Just before he closed his eyes for what he thought would be the last time, he saw a spaceship appear above him. He blinked several times, wondering if space mirages existed. But there it was, a ship. It was smaller than the one that had blown up the base, and it was smoother, softer to look at. Yet to Bill, it was just the same.

He snarled in righteous anger at the hateful aliens that had taken away his home, his people, and his pikelets. With the last of his strength, he raised his real arm and flipped them the bird.

"Fuck you, you fucking fuckers," he muttered. Apparently, he wasn't done with swearing quite yet. Quota be damned.

He expected the aliens to shoot a beam of green at him, just to finish what they'd failed to accomplish last time around.

On his last breath, Bill felt light-headed; his entire field of vision shimmered with a glow.

Then he discovered that life, or at least the unresolved bits, really did flash before your eyes when you believed you were going to die.

This must be what death is like, he thought before losing consciousness.

Chapter 4: Flashback

Bill Griffin had been a scrawny, anxious kid growing up. Beta when the world valued alphas, bookish and introverted at school while the loud, athletic boys got all the girls and attention. Of course, it didn't help that he wore glasses and had a prosthetic left hand and forearm due to an aberrant event when he was four. It gave the bullies something to target and made him feel like he would never fit in.

To make matters worse, the artificial extended hand was actually just a metal two-prong claw, a basic tool, really. Good enough to pick up a pencil and other small objects, but not useful for much else. Without a movable wrist, his range of motion was severely limited. Some kids thought his claw hand was cool, but most others treated him like a circus act, a veritable freak.

It wasn't until middle school that Bill received an upgrade. At least the new prosthetic looked more like a hand. But only the thumb and index finger were movable. The other three digits were there just for show, and the wrist remained fixed in a steadfast position. Upgrades were a luxury.

During those years, the best Bill could hope for was that the bullies would leave him alone for a few days, so he could recover between beatings. He spent most of his time in the school library or playing online games against and with people he never met. Virtual team players with names like Rex Krotos, Lord Roosevelt, and Bonny Bu.

And he spent significant hours hoping that the goddess Clarity Thomas would someday look his way, even if for a split second.

Clarity was the reason he'd tried out for the space program. She was a ten in anyone's books, tall, beautiful, and outgoing, with a winning smile and a determination that led her to surprising achievements. She was the object of Bill's fantasies, and she had been born with a free pass through life. If she'd wanted to cash it in, she could have made millions as a model or movie star, or even by simply marrying any old trillionaire and enjoying the luxury of wealth and power.

Instead, Clarity had spent as much time in the library as Bill, applying herself to the best of her abilities and graduating top of their class.

Bill had watched Clarity from a distance, admiring everything about her, from her fiery red hair through to the way she sat with such poise at her study desk. He never got up the courage to do much more than exchange the polite greetings of a passing acquaintance.

Except for that time when she dropped her notebook. Bill noticed it after he had watched her leave the library one Friday afternoon. He scooped it up, gathered his things, and ran after her, but he was too late. She was gone. He took the notebook, fully intending to ignore it until he saw her again.

The ignoring of the notebook part lasted until he got home, did his chores, and escaped to his room. Bill pulled it out of his backpack, stared at it until the guilt set in, and then put it back in the pack, zipping it closed. He tried studying, cleaning his room, and distracting himself with a new online game that held all manner of mystical monsters.

"LR, watch your six!" yelled Bill.

"Ouch!" responded Lord Roosevelt, deftly swinging the death blade a hundred and eighty degrees, effectively decapitating the Orc that had jumped out of its hiding hole. "What did I tell you about yelling into the mic?"

"Oh, sorry," said Bill, making his avatar shrug its shoulders.

The shrug command was useless for defense and offense, but Bill found it helpful when playing with more formidable gamers. It gave his avatar, Iron Fist, a way to show his humility, a trait that was important in alpha- and beta-team relationships. It was the only way a beta such as himself was allowed to play in the same arena as the alphas.

His gunplay and swordplay were average. His only redeeming quality was his skill as a tactician. Bill suspected that was the only reason that alpha gamers like Lord Roosevelt would allow him to partner with them. His shrugging gesture also seemed to de-escalate moments of ire when he failed to put down an enemy combatant at his partner's expense.

"You've been so good about losing that bad habit over the past few weeks," said Roosevelt. "What's gotten into you?"

"Sorry for being distracted. Can I tell you a secret?" asked Bill. His avatar's voice, so unlike his own, was deep and resonating with maturity. When gaming, Bill always adjusted the vocal monitor. He had to take confidence anywhere he could find it.

"Iron Fist, if you're thinking about breaking up the team to follow that Rex Krotos dick, then you better keep that secret to yourself. And stop apologizing so much. It makes you come across as weak," said Roosevelt, as he ran toward a castle that appeared on the horizon.

"Sorr— I mean, sure thing." Bill followed behind and took a moment to change up his weapon. The pause in conversation gave him some time to rephrase what he wanted to say. "You have experience with women, right?"

"Hell yeah," said Roosevelt. His voice was smooth and reassuring, like a late night audio jockey's. "Is that what this is all about? Why you've been distracted? You have a girly-girl crush?"

Bill blushed at Roosevelt's teasing and felt thankful that his avatar couldn't translate it for all to see.

"Ok, sure. Yeah," Bill said, trying not to stutter.

"Spill it. How long have you two been dating? What's her name?" prompted Roosevelt.

"Um, it's not like that," said Bill.

"Oh, my bad," said Roosevelt. "What's *his* name?"

"Oh. Ha. No. Nothing like that either," stuttered Bill. Regaining his composure, he said, "This is the thing. There's this really hot girl at my school who I really like. I'll just call her Clare, not her real name."

"Ok, so you want to know how to ask her out?" Roosevelt crossed the bridge toward the castle, blade at the ready.

"Well, sort of," responded Bill. "I just recently got an opportunity to find out more about her." His Iron Fist avatar followed Roosevelt into the castle.

"That's good. Getting some intel on your target is a good strategy."

"Well, that's just it. The information would be coming from — Whoa!" The suit of armor in the castle corridor had come alive and swung its axe toward Bill, causing him to react quickly by instinctively jumping aside.

Roosevelt swung his broad blade and promptly cut the armored figure through its midriff, earning their team an additional thousand points.

"Go for it. It can't hurt to find out more about Clare through her friends and what not," said Roosevelt just before he ducked through a hidden passageway, narrowly avoiding a deadly pendulum that suddenly swung down toward him.

Unfortunately for Bill, he saw the swinging pendulum too late and his avatar got decapitated by the blade's return swing, kicking him out of the game. But Bill wasn't too upset. He got the answer he wanted, choosing to focus on the *'what not'* that Roosevelt had provided and interpreting it to include sources like Clarity's notebook.

<<<>>>

Bill turned off the computer and silenced his comm-screen, as if he were being watched. He carefully unzipped his pack and removed the notebook. He ran his hands over it and lifted it to his face and he breathed in deeply. Her scent that lingered on the pages reminded him of lavender and lilacs.

He wondered briefly if she would be able to smell him once he returned the notebook. Again, he reverently rubbed his hands over the cover and back, hoping she would realize how carefully he was treating her property, how she could trust him to respect her belongings, that they were safe with him. She was safe with him.

Then he opened it and all manner of dreams unfolded. The pages were filled with purple-penned poetry and sketches, aspirations and hopes, and observations of specific fellow students and mankind as a whole. The spiral-bound pages were no longer a mere notebook, but a journal of sorts or more like a personal diary. It was a map into the mind and soul of Clarity.

Bill read through it and read it again. The notebook had only a dozen or so blank pages left. Clarity had worked diligently to capture bits of herself and her surrounding universe. And the combination was stunningly beautiful.

The more he read through this memoir in the making, the more he fell in love with her. Not satisfied with being just another pretty face like her mother and aunts, kept women who were provided for by rich husbands, Clarity wanted to be her own person. To gain the respect of her peers and superiors alike through hard work and study.

Near the end in a section titled *Hope Worthy*, he found his name buried in one little paragraph. *It's rather sad that Bill Griffin doesn't recognize his potential. There is something about him that intrigues me. An inner strength perhaps?*

That night, Bill slept very little. He looked in the mirror, he looked at his hand, and he looked at that notebook line that seared into his mind and heart. She had noticed him. Clarity knew who he was and thought he had potential. So much so, that she even found him intriguing. Bill Griffin, Loser Extraordinaire, who spent countless hours hiding in his room, gaming with strangers, had potential.

How could this perfect girl see him that way? How could he keep her intrigued?

Over the weekend, Bill read the notebook cover to cover several times. He memorized passages, sniffed the pages, and slept with the notebook under his pillow as if it would fill his dreams with possibilities.

He certainly couldn't return the notebook to her, not face to face. She couldn't find out he had read it.

Early Monday morning, Bill was at the library an hour before it opened, taking one last look at the notebook. As soon as the doors opened, he scurried to her desk and placed the notebook under a pile of books Clarity had been studying. She would never know.

Later, Bill found a purple pen in the bottom of his backpack. It must have been clipped to the notebook and had fallen off. He probably should return it, as well, but it was too late. She wouldn't miss it, would she?

Clarity was too busy being scathingly brilliant with all things academic and now poetry. Surely, she wouldn't think twice about a mere pen.

She also excelled at everything athletic, from gymnastics and kickboxing to fencing and firearms. Given her diverse potential, it wasn't a shock to anyone when she applied to the Outer Planets Academy and was chosen for the accelerated program.

Bill had agonized over the news when he'd found out. He'd always imagined that one day, a long time in the future, they might fatefully end up together. After all, she thought he had *potential*. But how would that happen if she was out somewhere in space and Bill was stuck on dreary old Earth?

He had taken a good, hard look at himself in the mirror. Academically, he was near the top of his class. His only other skill was that he excelled at online games, particularly when it came to devising ways to best overpower opponents. But physically? He had the physique of a ghoul.

Bill was tall, and his face would be okay once his acne cleared up, if his acne cleared up. But he was still scrawny and weak. And nothing about growing up could take care of his glasses or prosthetic hand.

Bill didn't need to be told that he wasn't a good candidate for any space mission, potential be damned.

So, he got to work, keeping thoughts of Clarity at the forefront of every decision. At the time, he still lived in the grotty basement of his aunt's home that she shared with her on-again, off-again boyfriend, but they didn't pay too much attention to him, so he could come and go as he pleased.

He was determined to live up to Clarity's opinion of him. He stopped gaming. Every day for six months, he left his basement early so he could work out. He juggled three part-time jobs, as a dishwasher, a factory line grunt, and the toilet cleaner at a local club, all to save up enough money for corrective eye surgery.

And while he couldn't do anything about his hand, by the end of that six months, he was no longer the same weak, insecure gamer-kid who'd been continually harassed.

He walked into the local recruitment office for off-world assignments and pleaded with the officer in charge, expecting nothing more than disappointment.

Luckily for him, the entire space industry was on a public relations blitz. He managed to pass the physical requirements, and his prosthetic hand made him just the sort of recruit the marketing department was hoping to showcase. Bill was featured in a puff piece explaining how every average or below-average citizen could contribute to the space initiative.

Bill didn't care about the politics that had for once worked in his favor. He had simply been ecstatic. Beyond fucking thrilled. He'd whooped and hollered and jumped up and down, and a few years later, he graduated as a maintenance engineer. The least of all things he could possibly have been. Effectively, a space janitor, emphasis on space.

Clarity Thomas had long since departed for a plum assignment as second in command of the new base on some asteroid belt. Bill's first assignment was to support the growing lunar colony.

That's right. He was going to the moon. It was still a few million miles from where he wanted to be, yet he couldn't help but feel lucky. It was, he thought happily, a step in the right direction.

As long as he played along, he was promised his application to serve on the base in the asteroid belt would be given serious consideration. He was consigned to the Lunar Maintenance Service for two years of space labor, and in exchange, Bill would receive free room and board, a generous bi-weekly credit stipend, a bonus if he met certain performance metrics, and a fully operational prosthetic.

Bill hoped the new hand and arm combo would make Clarity see him in a new light. With all five movable fingers and a flexible wrist, he felt almost whole again.

But then, a few short weeks later, the Earth exploded, showering burning rocks and debris over the moon buggy, the base, and over Bill himself. It was not a fucking good day to die.

Or so he thought.

Chapter 5: Alien

When he dared to crack an eye open, Bill was in darkness and extremely confused.

Am I dead? Is this what the afterlife is like?

Only a dim light shone from the ceiling at the opposite side of the room. He tentatively reached out his hand from where it had fallen asleep and touched it to his face. An act of curiosity, a pinch in a dream.

He was, indeed, still alive. He raised himself up on his elbow, and the whole bed he had been sleeping on took a slow-arced swing. His surroundings didn't look anything like what he was used to on the lunar base. Besides, wasn't it destroyed? Where was he, if not the afterlife?

Looking up into the shadowed darkness, Bill saw the cables that suspended him from the ceiling. His bed was more of a porch swing, the kind his grandmother had on her old Victorian at the lake. Used to have.

Ah, Gram. Gone, like all the rest of them.

None of that, not now, imbecile!

He propped himself up and swung his legs out over the side of the swaying bed. Soft lighting gradually turned on from recessed channels along the walls. His movement must have triggered the sensors for the lights.

Where the hell am I? Remaining still for a moment, Bill detected a low hum all around him. The air smelled and felt different, as if processed through a filter. He was definitely on board a spaceship. But why? The shimmering light he had experienced before losing consciousness must have been some wild-ass transport technology.

After hopping off the bed, he realized that he was completely naked.

"What the hell." He squinted and scanned the room for his suit but felt a fast rush of adrenaline when he heard a high-pitched squeak beneath him.

"Pocket?"

Bill tried to focus and his eyes, getting used to the darkness, caught just a flash of white, along with the scratchy sound of feet. Like rat feet? He spotted his suit, folded neatly under his bed, his helmet placed carefully next to it, and then another quick glimpse of white. Maybe feathers?

"Pocket? Pocket!"

Again with the pockets?

"Who's there?" Bill asked, suddenly feeling self-conscious. He covered his junk with his good hand and lifted his prosthetic in front of his face. And then he remembered. His hand was all fucked up. Two of the fingers had been ripped off back on the moon, and the pinky was now bent at an impossible angle.

"Pocket!" A lump underneath Bill's suit started bouncing, then dragging the suit just a centimeter at a time across the room. Now, instead of an excited chirp, whatever was under the suit was chanting, slow and steady like a member of a crew team. "Pocket… pocket… pocket."

"Okay, I'll bite one more time. What. The. Fuck."

The suit stopped moving, and Bill held his breath as a bundle of white landed beside him. Bill swallowed as he watched. It was maybe a monkey? Maybe a stuffed animal on some kind of hyperkinetic power, placed as a sentry over the captive? The thing had eyes the size of walnuts, big and brown with lashes. Its arms were webbed triangles, and instead of hands, it had a number of claws. And its fur wasn't really fur; it was more like the feather boas a burlesque stripper would wrap around her, hiding all the parts you most wanted to see.

Just as he was thinking that, Bill jerked back and gave a muffled shout when the creature jumped straight up in the air and landed on Bill's shoulder.

"Pocket? No pocket."

Bill looked into the thing's eyes and watched as the feather fur slowly changed from white to what could best be described as flesh. Caucasian skin. Exactly the color of Bill's skin.

"What in hell?" Bill still covered his privates with his good hand, but he used the messed-up prosthetic to shoo the thing away. Every time he poked at it, it jumped up and over the stump.

"No. Pocket. One. Pocket. Po-Qeet. So-sweet." The creature smiled and showed its teeth, rows upon rows of teeth, all the color of Bill's skin. It was smiling, and playing jump rope like kids in a playground, making stupid rhymes and losing its breath. Finally, Bill used his good hand to grab the thing around the neck, but just as his fingers tightened, it fluttered its wings and squawked. Then it disappeared. Thin air disappeared. Like poof magic.

Bill slithered over the edge of the swinging bed and onto the floor, reaching for his moon suit. The gravity on the ship was slightly off from what he was used to on the moon and so his reach fell short of its target. Consciously readjusting for the weight differential of his arm, he managed to snag the right sleeve of the suit. Why the hell had someone taken off his clothes and left him on that bed naked, anyway?

He stood and slipped his feet into the bulky suit, noting with a grim smile that he was going commando. He would have preferred his underpants and regular under-suit gear, but they were missing. At least someone had left the suit.

"Pocket prize!"

Bill turned toward the voice and fell down, his feet tangled up in the suit. When he looked up, there was the creature-thing, hanging from the underside of the bed, swinging lazily. Bill squinted and realized that it had once again changed colors, this time sporting a body of shiny chrome feather-fur.

"Pocket prize," it whispered, and carefully reached into a pouch right on its abdomen, pulling out a purple pen. Slowly, its whole body turned that same shade of purple, and it gave Bill a big purple-toothed grin.

"Hey, you little fucker! That's mine! Well, it's not really mine, but it's mine until I return it to the owner! Hand it over, Creep!"

"Not Creep! Qeet! I Qeet! Like Sweet!"

Bill pulled his suit up his legs and stood again. "Wait, so your name is actually Qeet? Rhymes with, um."

"Treat! Feet! Meat! Qeet! Pocket Prize for Qeet!"

"Well, fine, then," Bill said, zipping up his suit. "Qeet. I'm Bill. And that, new pal, if you *are* in fact a pal and not a gal, is my pen." He reached for his only tangible memory of Earth, his Clarity.

The Qeet creature fluttered its wings and squawked almost like a chicken before it promptly disappeared.

"Hey! Little Fuck! Give that back, or I'll—"

"Qeet pal. Not gal." It was barely a whisper, then a little chirp from above that made Bill crane his neck. Now Qeet hung from the ceiling, and Bill could barely make out the little sucker's feet. How could he hang upside down like that? The creature looked at Bill, licking the pen and taunting him. Qeet opened his mouth in T-Rex fashion as if to chomp on the purple stylus.

Trying not to provoke Qeet anymore than he had, Bill considered a gentler approach.

"Ok, so we're pals, then. Best buds, if you want. But Qeet, you have to listen. That thing is special to me! I've never even used it before. Never even taken the cap off the damn thing! It belongs to a really special girl, a girl I hope to find one day so that I can return it to her. Look, it's been the worst day ever, little guy. And it's probably not going to get better, the way my life is going."

Qeet tilted his head, seemingly responding to Bill's words. At least the creature didn't put the pen in his mouth. Instead, he held the purple pen and started rocking it in his arms like a baby. With a popping sound from his feet, Qeet somersaulted down from the ceiling to land on Bill's head.

Sighing with relief, Bill extended his good hand.

"Come on. Um, Qeet? Please?"

Slowly, Qeet's feathers changed to dark brown, and he stretched himself over to look directly into Bill's eyes, upside down.

"Sorry, sorry. Qeet return memory to Bill." He slid the pen down to land in Bill's good hand. With a furry raised eyebrow, he examined Bill's damaged hand. "What what?"

"Yeah, see, I'm not in a real chatty mood right now, so I'm not gonna explain my what-what to a crazy animal alien." Bill hid the stump behind his back.

"Ha! Kimra have new puzzle to play!"

"Who the hell is Kim—" Bill looked up from the purple pen when he heard a flutter of wings and a squawk, but Qeet had disappeared again.

And though he didn't like to admit it, Bill felt even lonelier than he had before.

Chapter 6: Loving the Aliens

Surely there would be a door. Bill had spent at least an hour scouring the walls of his prison, feeling along in the semi-darkness for some sign of a seam, a knob, a button, anything that would indicate an exit. He had already looked for a 'this way out' neon sign. He took a break when his stomach interrupted the silence, by starting with a low rumble, then growing to almost a piercing scream, the sound of a far-away rabbit shrieking when his aunt's cat finally landed on it.

He smiled at the sad memory and slouched down against the wall. At least whoever his captors were had had the decency to leave his suit, pack, and helmet, now his only true possessions in the universe. Besides the purple pen.

"Sure could use some food, here," he said, rubbing his stomach. "Pikelets would go nice about now. With those little nipple-shaped chocolate morsels, maybe? Or strawberries, all slathered with whipped cream? No, no, let's have them encrusted with cinnamon, with crunchy slivers of almonds, yes?"

He stood and tentatively felt along what he thought might be a crack in the wall. Knocked politely. Tap tap tap.

"Hello? Bill Griffin, here. Just checking in. Not sure of the time, sorry if I'm waking anyone." Then he stopped and smirked. "Not in Mayberry anymore, now, are we, Otis?"

He started hammering on the door, or what he thought to be the door, with his fucked-up hand, smashing the thumb and the only remaining good fingers again and again and raising his voice with each powerful knock.

"HELLLLLLOOO? Some toast, maybe? Toast? What am I even saying? I AM TOAST, RIGHT??? You're all snickering into your hands, paws, or whatever right now, listening to me, right? Getting your laughs in at the broken little human you found cowering on the moon on his break from his fucking janitorial job, right? Well, I've got news for you folks. Bill Griffin is a lot tougher than he looks, you can bet your ASSES! A LOT TOUGHER."

His voice caught in the back of his throat and he was glad he was alone for the moment, wiping that single tear off of his cheek. Christ.

Tssssst.

Bill turned and bit his lip as a portion of the wall on the opposite side of the room slid open and the tallest woman-like creature he had ever laid eyes on slithered into the room.

Or at least, it seemed like a slither. She stood at least seven feet tall, like professional basketball-player tall, and as she moved toward him, his eyes blinded by the light behind her, he squinted to be sure it was actually a woman.

Oh, but it was. Most certainly a woman. Tall, yes, but as his eyes grew accustomed to the new light, Bill's lips parted in wonder. His breath caught in his throat.

She had eyes bigger than the 'okay' sign you make with your thumb and your index finger, if you are lucky enough to have those digits. And her pupils were vertical, slices of black against yellow irises.

As she drew closer and bent down toward Bill's face, the pupils enlarged like wedges of pie, and he noticed that her eyebrows were raised, and the hairs on them weren't hairs at all, but spikes of skin. He pulled back as far as the wall behind him would allow.

Her skin was yellow, like really yellow, yellow crayon yellow. The yellow was the color you get when you cross a canary with a ripe lemon. And there were tattoos, or at least what looked like tattoos, all over her body, very regularly spaced in octagons of reddish brown.

He felt a compulsion to reach out and touch that skin. Was it silky? Scaly? Or more like suede?

The weird part, if there could be a weird part when juxtaposed with yellow skin and slits for pupils, was her nose. A perfect human nose, delicate with nostrils flaring, tentatively testing the air around him. Something about the nose threw Bill back to a memory, but he couldn't put a finger on it. Certainly not with one of his lost fingers, and certainly not on scary snake-woman's nose.

She blinked and reached out with an elegant yellow arm to touch him, and when she did, his suit with its fabric, integrated electronics, polymer-metal gaskets, and all just faded right away. It didn't fall to the ground. It didn't melt. It just faded right off his body.

And once again, Bill Griffin was naked.

Is this it? Is this the part where I die naked where I stand?

Not knowing what to expect and what to do next, he covered himself. As he did, he got a good look at her legs. Her thighs came up to his chest, rising from the floor like the strong but sculpted roots of that sycamore tree in his aunt's front yard. He watched, slack jawed as she flexed the muscles in her calves. It reminded him of the time they'd gone to Florence and stood before the David. Glorious, huge, rippling muscles.

Only hers were yellow and brown snakeskin. She was fucking spectacular.

Bill cleared his throat after sucking back in drool and swallowing hard. "Um. Hello."

She blinked but didn't answer.

"I was just wondering, and sorry if I interrupted whatever you might have been doing, but I was wondering if it might be possible to get something to eat?" The least they could do was grant him a last meal before they executed him.

She blinked again.

"Usually I would shake hands before asking for something, but, well." He held up his prosthetic, which now, after having the shit beaten out of it against the wall, was even more pathetic, wires springing out from fingers, fingers just barely hanging on. "And, of course, my regular 'shaking' hand is, uh, otherwise occupied."

She looked down to where he hid his awkwardly growing member and the first hint of a smile spread over her face, thin-lipped but not menacing. She once again lifted a graceful arm and waved her hand over the seam where Bill had been pounding and a door slid open to reveal a small room with a toilet. Inside was a pile of what looked like clothes. Bill slid his hand over the unfamiliar feather-light fabric, feeling its cool smoothness.

This was a good sign. Perhaps they weren't going to kill him. At least not yet.

"Well, hey now," Bill said, and he turned to her with a little bow. "Thank you so much. I needed that toilet. Somewhere to pee and a pile of clothes. Who could ask for anything more?" He backed up into the comfort chamber, not wanting her to see his crack, and watched the giant of a woman wave her arm again. The door slid closed.

"I could, actually," he muttered to himself. "I could ask for something more. Like pikelets."

Dressed and relieved, he knocked politely, and the door swished open.

"Thanks again. What do you think?" He spread his arms out, showing her his new clothes that actually fit him well and were so comfortable he had almost cried again in that cramped little room.

She was on his bed, lying there stretched out, one leg swinging over the edge, the other spread out luxuriously in front of her. Her arms were up over her head and she seemed like a woman just rising after a long nap. When he walked toward the bed, she rose and held out a closed fist to him. He put his good hand under it, and she dropped a writhing insect of some kind into his palm.

It had too many legs to count and was about as big as an average barn mouse. Bill closed his fist and looked up at her.

"Eat," she said.

"Ah, you speak! Nice first word. But really? Eat this thing? It's still, um, alive."

"Eat. Tasty."

"You're kidding, right?"

She remained silent, staring at him with those hypnotic eyes.

"Okay, I get it. You're *not* kidding."

Bill thought back to survival videos he used to watch on Earth, lonely people deserted in harsh climates, left to live or die. Those guys were completely bonkers, eating all sorts of weird shit, gross bugs and snails just for the calories. At least what was being offered to him wasn't half as bad as what those survivalists had to eat. There was no guarantee that Bill would get another chance at another meal. Besides, he had read that insects were packed full of protein.

He opened his hand and lifted it to his lips as he watched the thing crawl around. "Well. I *am* hungry, after all. Maybe if I kill it first?"

"Just eat," she said, and she made that sound, the *tsssst* sound he'd heard when she first came in the room.

"Well, seeing as I'm fairly sure this might be my last meal, it might as well be a funny one, right?" he asked, and with his eyes wide open, staring right into her slit eyes, he popped part of the sucker into his mouth and bit down on half of it, thinking all the while of chocolate. Both halves, now separated, continued to squirm in his mouth and in his hand.

Bill closed his eyes while he chomped away. It was crunchy on the outside and gooey on the inside. As the mashed-up-insect-saliva mix washed over his taste buds, Bill opened his eyes in surprise.

"Mmm, hey!" he said with a smile. "That wasn't half as bad as I'd thought it would be, mmm." He popped the remaining part of the uneaten insect into his mouth and chewed enthusiastically.

"What's your name, anyway?" Bill asked, as some gooey bit of chewed-up insect came flying out of his mouth, hitting the snake lady on one of her perfect breasts, a delightful orb that made him want to trace the snake pattern, with his good hand, of course. He quickly covered his mouth with his hand.

Ignoring Bill's bad manners, she tilted her head down. In one smooth motion, her tongue flicked out from her mouth and licked off the offending morsel from her breast. Then she looked up at Bill and answered, "Rikki. I am Rikki."

"No. Stop it," Bill said. "You mean like the mongoose? Rikki Tikki Tikki or something? Little dude that kills snakes? Kipling? Ring a bell?" He let himself snort out a laugh, but she stopped him with a wide-eyed glare.

"Just an Earth joke," he said. "Location, location, you know. Hey, who's Kimra? Let's change the subject, right?"

"Kimra waitsss," Rikki said. She gave him a tight little smile and turned to lead him out of the room.

"Well, okay, then." He followed her with eyes fixated on her ass as it swayed with her smooth walk. She wore a gauzy yellow thing, he saw now. It matched the yellow skin but was a thicker material in the places on her body that he most wanted to watch. It was thin enough to see Rikki's undulating waist and those incredible legs as they sauntered ahead of him.

Nothing wrong with a little imaginative play on the day you die. Might as well have fun while you can. And PS? I can't remember the last time my mind got to wander up and down legs like this. Oh, right, never.

As if she could read his mind, Rikki stopped and twisted around, lowering her torso so that she could look into his eyes. He felt his mouth go dry.

"Still right here, trying to keep up! Off to meet the Kimra, right?" He gave his best, most disarming little boy smile and shrugged.

"Tssssst," she sighed, and led him through a maze of hallways and arched thresholds to rooms where all kinds of creatures, strange but strangely beautiful, were busy at work.

"Is everyone on board female besides me and maybe Qeet?" he asked Rikki's beautifully muscled glutes. She didn't answer, so he fastened his attention to the glimpses of the aliens as they glided past.

Some were winged, some were furry, and Bill could have sworn they passed one that, heavy with obvious pregnancy, had udders, six or seven breast-like things, exposed and pink and dangling for all the world to see. He was afraid to blink, there were so many to catch sight of while Rikki walked at a furiously liquid zippy pace.

Whatever they were doing, it was obvious to Bill that they were preparing for something. Everyone seemed to be busy with a task, whether it was reinforcing a bulkhead, inspecting the life support systems, or testing equipment that did who knows what. Bill was sure there was a lot more going on than he could see.

Even though the women on the ship were alien to him, for some reason, they all reminded Bill of Earth. Or perhaps someone he knew on Earth. Bill couldn't exactly put his finger on what it was. He chuckled to himself as he looked at his prosthetic hand and the misaligned appendages.

Of course, you can't put a finger on it, Idiot. Your fingers are all fucked-up, for Earth's sake. Or at least for the memory of Earth.

As Bill continued to gawk at the women, he felt a visceral response within his loins and he thought of Clarity. His Clarity, whom he never got the chance to tell how much she meant to him. And now, he probably never would. The sadness overwhelmed him, and Bill closed his eyes in sorrow.

When Rikki stopped, Bill nearly ran into her, so engulfed in angst. She made her *tssssst* sound and motioned for him to enter a room that was nearly empty.

Empty, that is, except for the vision of perfection that must, please God let it be, Kimra. Awe trumped sadness every time.

Chapter 7: Blinded Me with Science

She stood in the corner of the room, radiating light and color, and she reminded Bill Griffin of every shiny new car he never had. Her hair was jet black with tinselly blue highlights and was pulled into an efficient bun at the base of her neck. She wore a foil-like skirt, short and tightly wrapped around her body, and she looked like a ready-to-bake Idaho potato in the corner grocery store back home. She also looked like she could jump into a packed gladiator arena and be the last one standing. She looked delicious and dangerous all wrapped in one efficient package.

"Have you also had a mouth injury? Besides the hand job, I mean?" She gave him just a ghost of a smile as he pulled his jaw up and closed his lips.

"No, I… no." He glanced at Rikki in a futile attempt to gain support, but she was lazily testing the air with her tongue. He had seen her use her tongue earlier when he spit out that morsel of insect chow on her breast. But this time, he was able to see it more clearly. Her tongue wasn't forked, exactly, but this was a new observation, this long, skinny, pointed tongue that seemed to have a mind of its own. She caught him staring at her, pulled it back into her mouth, and blinked one eye.

"Kimra isss ssseeing you now," Rikki said, and she turned on her foot and slither-swayed out of the room.

"Bill, is it? They call me Kimra, as I am sure you have surmised by now. Come, come." She motioned for him to get up on a chrome pallet that had slid out from the wall.

"You want me to get on that?" asked Bill. He shivered as he ran his hand over the smooth surface. "It's cold."

"You will become acclimatized to it," said Kimra, motioning again for Bill to hoist himself up.

He climbed the steps to it and swiveled to sit facing her, legs dangling from the edge. He felt goose bumps rise along his body as the cold from the metal pallet cut through the thin fabric of his pants. She pressed a button and looked at the controls on a pedestal that protruded from the wall, her brow wrinkled in concentration.

He thought suddenly of Clarity again, studying in the library, tongue clenched between her teeth, brow furrowed and concentrated on the task at hand. Bill dry swallowed.

"Look right here," she said, and she pointed to her left ear. Her nails were painted blue, perfectly shaped, and buffed. As he looked at her left ear lobe, she leaned toward him and shone a light into each eye. Her eyes were electric blue like her nails, and distant. She smelled of something that he was struggling to place. Something medicinal, maybe? Or used for cleaning?

Something the oldsters used to have tucked away in the garage or broom closet?

"WD-40!" he pronounced finally.

"I do not understand." She leaned away from him, collapsing her little flashlight and placing it in the breast pocket of her foil garb.

"You smell like WD-40. It was a valuable staple to Uncle Al's tool bench." he said, breathing in the smell of well-oiled machines, hinges that don't squeak anymore, bike spokes.

"I want to say thank you but am not completely certain about that being a fully appropriate response." She moved like a machine, too, Bill thought as he watched her pressing lights on his chrome slab. After tapping a series of different colored areas, her arm shot back into place at her side.

Was she machine or was she humanoid? Or maybe a cross of the two? Her perfect body had all the best human dimensions. He licked his lips as her foiled breasts nearly touched his arm. She pulled some flat steel bands from the sides of the pallet, carefully arranging them beside Bill's legs.

"Recline, please." That little ghost smile came to her mouth again but didn't reflect in her eyes, which seemed to change like the aurora borealis. Maybe not human after all.

He lay back on the pallet, again feeling the cold permeate his clothing. "So," he said, "Are you Doctor Kimra?"

"I am a healer, of sorts, yes."

"You're planning on healing me?" This was very good news. Healing meant no killing, right?

"I am planning on examining your vessel, its external surface, and its portals to your organs. And, of course, there are dramatic issues regarding your appendage here." She touched his mangled hand with a pointed fingernail.

A snapping sound made Bill jerk to attention. He looked down at those appendages Kimra had mentioned and realized she had pressed a light or button that controlled the metal bands. Now, they wrapped around his biceps and thighs like those ancient metal bracelets little girls used to wear, snapped snug and secure and definitely not about to let him go anywhere soon.

"What the—"

"Hmm," interrupted Kimra. "We need a stable plane, so must restrain the physical vessel. We will not damage or impair you. Fear not."

Bill watched her face as she spoke, fascinated even while terror made a slow crawl from his gut to his chest. She spoke in a hum of a voice, low and sultry but with almost a touch of hairdryer in the background, like a soft faraway buzz.

Her lips were thin and not treated. No lipstick, no gloss. Her eyelashes were long, obviously not real. Her hair pulled her eyes back so much that she looked like she might be in pain. Should be in pain, at least.

"Do you wear your hair like that every day? Looks like it might give you a headache," Bill said, his mouth dry and his eyes blinking as he tried to keep the growing panic at bay.

"Explain these stubbles of hair that grow about your facial orifice, please." She was close, so close he could have picked up his head from that table and touched his tongue to her little lips, but she wasn't looking *at* him. She was really looking at his parts, looking *through* him.

"Oh, well, yeah. Lots of commotion these days, haven't had the opportunity to shave." He tried a chuckle, but it came out as a dry snort. "Apologies to the hostess."

She moved down to loosen his shirt and he grasped at straws. "So, are you allowed to tell me where we are right now? And what I've gotten myself into this time? Because you know, people always said I just seem to get myself into the darnedest situations. And here we are! So where are we, exactly?"

"Breathe deeply and be silent," she said, placing the end of a long filament of metal to his chest. It tickled along both of his nipples and he felt goosebumps rise along his chest and arms.

"Do you have a captain here? Can you take me to your leader? Get it? Like in old movies before vids?" Bill licked his lips again. "Any way a guy could get a drink around here? I'm thirsty as a hound dog after a hunt. Has anyone ever told you that you look like a goddess? Like you could just wave your hand and make it rain?" Bill knew he was babbling, but what's a guy to do when terror runs the show?

"Do you understand the word, silent?" Kimra asked, still dragging that little filament over his chest, now down to his navel. "Your questions will receive the attention they deserve when your physical vessel has commenced its permutation process."

"Huh?"

Another shadowed smile, but this time Kimra actually looked into his eyes.

"You must, for now, Bill Griffin, be silent. I beg." As soon as her words were spoken, Kimra stood up and cocked her head, her eyes once again focused on the faraway. She held her hand up to him in a 'stop' motion. Bill held his breath, watching as she nodded her head, as if listening to someone else, as if she were having a conversation inside her head.

When she returned to her examination, she seemed preoccupied. Methodically, she chopped at his knees to get a reflex, making that little soft humming noise.

"Wait," Bill whispered. "What was that all about? What just happened?"

She raised her head and whispered back, "I needed to process an incoming message."

"Huh? What message?" asked Bill.

"It was an internal communication. What you would call, telepathic," answered Kimra, with a matter-of-fact demeanor.

"You can do that?" Bill said incredulously, his eyebrows raised. "I would think that would cause great problems, having voices in your head." He continued to watch her metal-wrapped body and blue-tipped fingers as she handled his legs and feet. "How do you filter out the noise?"

Kimra continued her humming, absent-minded and almost indecipherable.

"By sharing all knowledge, we collectively become as one. We are in constant development of a base of information and experience which grows, in part, by any incoming visitor or new cluster member."

"Like the old Wiki concept?" Bill leaned forward for a good whiff of WD-40.

"In most recent research, like your human star show's Borg, if you followed that one."

"I did! I watched the vids on those when I was a kid!" Bill stopped himself then and went on with just a note of trepidation. "Wait, didn't the Borg turn everyone into the same thing? Wasn't that like a goal, for everyone to have the exact frame of reference as everyone else? Hey, wait, are you assimilating me?" He became alarmed when her blue fingertips wrapped around his prosthetic hand in a firm, controlling grip.

"No, that Borg business is sheer nonsense. Drivel. I'm simply injecting mecphages into your lifestream. In order to connect you to the cluster consciousness. To gain understanding of the galactic tongue. "

"Wait a minute, did you say McPhages? Like drive-through fast food?"

"No, Bill Griffin, I said mecphages."

"So, MacPhages, which are more like bagpipe-toting, skirt-wearing, ax-wielding, robot clansman wreaking havoc on my innards?"

"Bill Griffin, your penchant to Earthsplain technology is counterproductive. Would mechanical phages be more comforting to your seemingly damaged psyche?”

“Nah, that’s too long, I’m good with mecphages. Carry on.”

“And this?” She switched her focus to her grip on his prosthetic. “This simply is refuse, or garbage, if you will. Surely you understand that,” she said, with as close to a scoff as he’d seen from her. “You retain only two working phalanges on this apparatus.”

“Well, I’ve been working around that little handicap just fine, really.”

“It is primitive, and though it may have served a purpose in the distant past, it is time for an upgrade, my new Earthling friend.”

And for the first time, Kimra gave Bill a shiny platinum smile, and her eyes had just a trace of true laughter in their cosmic depths. In one smooth motion, she twisted the prosthetic and ripped it off.

Of course, it didn’t actually hurt. That wasn’t the point. But Bill howled anyway, just threw his head back and howled like a boy in a playground whose ball has been stolen by the resident bully. The memory of losing his real arm and the overwhelming shock that followed short-circuited his mind.

And while he was passing out, he distinctly heard her sing familiar words of what seemed a very, very old rap song. Daft someone, Bill thought in his subconscious mind. Maybe Punk. But not quite right, almost a mashup with some vid series about a part-machine man with superpowers. Something about “Earthling, we can rebuild you with our technology.

Twerk it, fake it, do-do-do it, mecphage it, Borg better, Borg stronger, Borg faster. Twerk it."

Chapter 8: Put Yo Hands Up

The pain in his arm was familiar, of course. Traumatic pain imprints on a kid's soul, and the initial loss of his left forearm was most certainly the clearest and most horrific memory of Bill's childhood. But there was an emotional pain, as well. Childhood melted into those awful teen years, and Bill's left hand, or the lack of it, became the primary source of his social humiliation. Or at least that was how he remembered it.

Scenes from a playground, panic in a tidal pool on vacation, a skateboard incident on the street, all of those memories hurt physically as a result of the accident; the emotional pain, though, happened almost daily, and to Bill it was the go-to excuse for his withdrawal into gaming in the dark recesses of his aunt's basement.

By far the most painful of those memories was at the Graduation Ball on that last fated day of high school. It was also Bill's most cherished moment with Clarity.

As he lay on Kimra's table and surrendered to oblivion, that day came blasting forward into his very resistant memory. He felt his lip muscles twitch in revulsion, swimming in the memory of a song by that long-ago band.

<<◇>>

Alone at the Grad Ball, Bill listened to the band struggle with a popular song, something about a space highway. His eyes never rested, darting from the Grand Hall's back door to the swinging door of the women's rest room. He waited, of course, for Clarity. Just the thought of laying eyes on the most beautiful girl in the school, the town, the world, gave him a lump in his throat.

As always, he was invisible to his fellow students, but by now that didn't even hit his radar. They were all dressed to the hilt, some in tuxedos and some in freshly bought or at least pressed suits, and the women wore sexy dresses and a cacophony of flowery, citrusy perfumes. He felt just the touch of a headache coming on.

He wore his best suit, which was also his only suit. In this lighting, its cuffs didn't look that frayed, and he had mastered a stealthy technique of tugging at them to make it less noticeable that his arms stuck out a bit too much. He'd worn black socks so that the pants, just a tad short, didn't call too much attention to themselves, either. Aunt Em had coached him on the smart ways to cover his wardrobe issues and had made too big a deal about how handsome he looked when he had finally stood at the front door for her approval. He knew she was biased, but something in him still clutched at those straws.

All he wanted was a moment alone with Clarity. Maybe a dance. Since she'd written in her journal that he had 'potential,' that meant she had done a fair amount of thinking about him, right? Didn't she also mention that she found him intriguing? Surely, she'd dance with him, at least?

He watched as someone covertly dumped another bottle of booze into the punch on the refreshment table next to him. That shit had to be pretty potent by now. He smiled at the girl who'd done the deed, but she looked right through him on her way back to the dance floor.

Mean girl number 27, Bill thought, letting his smile fade. He watched her join her beautiful friends on the dance floor, their hands above their heads holding cups of boozy fruit punch.

Suddenly, he felt it. A definite surge in psychic energy hit him every time Clarity entered the room. He looked up at the door, his mouth dropping open at the sight of her, all wrapped in some shiny kind of blue material, her red hair cascading over her shoulders.

She was laughing, and he was beguiled by the contrast between the whiteness of her teeth and the perfectly applied red lipstick. Just as Bill thought about getting some of that crazy punch, his glance rested on the sleaze ball who clutched Clarity's upper arm. Studying her face, Bill realized that Clarity was only feigning a laugh. Her eyes told a different story. No, she was almost wincing, like she regretted being there with her date.

Bill's stomach lurched. Should he react without knowing for sure what the situation was?

The sleaze was Chad Barkly, quarterback and all-around Prom King kind of guy. He had been, in fact, Prom King, to Clarity's Queen, just this past spring.

They hadn't even gone together as a date to the prom; it had just been a stupid, perfectly stupid, coincidence, and was only one of the things that made Bill hate everything about this guy. No one deserved the kind of luck Chad Barkly had received over the course of his high-school career.

The whole crowning thing at the prom had apparently been enough to spark some kind of hormonal romance, because from April until now, Chad and Clarity, or the "Double C's," as Chad called them to his locker-room audience, were now a *thing*.

A thing that made Bill Griffin's blood boil. Enough so that he decided to go stag to the Grad Ball, after convincing himself that he could certainly have gotten some girl to say yes to him, with the sole purpose of getting a moment alone with Clarity to tell her that he cared. Yes, he would work up the nerve, and he would just spout off the truth, dammit, loud and confident, without stuttering or choking up.

Clarity would soon be gone, training at the Outer Planets Academy. He couldn't let the summer slip by without telling her how he stayed up nights thinking about her. He had to have that moment. And somehow, everything would just slip into place.

Just as Bill started to make his way toward Clarity, he actually did just that. He slipped on some of the mean girls' punch and bumped into the same one who had spiked the bowl. Her cup sloshed up and over, and the next thing he knew, there was a cupful of red punch on the crotch of his pants.

"Way to go, Loser," said mean girl 27, as she and her friends stopped dancing and looked at his crotch.

"Yeah, looks like you finally got some action, Billy Bob," said another, a mean girl he'd never numbered.

"Were you maybe thinking about a little of this?" said still another. She turned her back to him and lifted her dress to display the first real bare ass Bill had ever seen. Like, no underwear, just this perfect round ass.

Bill's mouth went dry and his face got hot and in his stupor he could not for the life of him take his eyes off that ass.

They started laughing then, and one of them even dared to reach out to take Bill's prosthetic hand, guiding it over to the ass to stroke it.

He almost vomited. God, how much more horrific it might have been, he thought to himself later, as he played this memory over and over again in his mind.

Mortified, he somehow found his way out of the ballroom, trying his very best to not hear other students laughing at him, trying his very best not to see them pointing at his crotch, which, in the aftermath of the perfect ass visual, was still embarrassingly tented.

"Fuck," he muttered, just as he failed to negotiate the steps outside of the hall. He tripped and fell, catching himself with the prosthetic, which took the brunt of his weight. Bill gave up, just decided to sit his ass down right where he was. He assessed the damage: as usual, it was mostly emotional. The hand was a little scratched up, maybe a bit misaligned, but it was his spirit that had taken the true blow.

He couldn't even drive himself home from here. Most of the kids in his school had their own transports, took for granted the riches of their parents or grandparents, spent their teenage weekends cruising around together.

"Not me, though, right? Can't give poor old Bill Griffin his own ride. Nope, No Sir. Good for your character, to have to save up for it yourself." He looked up at the clock tower across the street and sighed. The dance had barely begun, and here he was, getting ready to call good old Aunt Em to come and save him from the monsters of high school.

And then he felt it. Smelled it. All of his senses rose to attention. A hand rested on his shoulder, and the smell of lavender filled his nostrils. He tipped his head up and there she was. Like some kind of magic fairy.

Clarity smiled down at him, then took a seat on the stairs. He started to protest, because of her fancy dress, but no words came out. He must have been blushing because he could feel the heat on his cheeks.

"I saw you stumble down the stairs. Are you okay?" she asked. He looked into her eyes, the closest they had ever been to his face except for in his dreams, and they looked so genuine, so concerned, so very, very, smart. And maybe? Maybe just a little bit sad.

Finally, he found his voice. This was his moment! He would not fuck this up! Despite his embarrassment, he let a smile spread across his face.

"Oh, sure. Uh… I'm okay. Leftie here has seen better nights, but I'm all in one piece." He held up his pathetic fake hand and showed her its new scratches. He forced a chuckle past the lump in his throat.

"Looks painful. But I'm sure you're a better judge of that than I am. I brought you this," she said, holding up some wet paper towels. "Saw your spill, too. Rough night so far, huh?" She smiled, and he could have sworn it was a little shy. "You should try to get to some club soda, I think. Or maybe it's detergent and vinegar?"

Her forehead wrinkled up and her eyes turned upward and to the left, in total concentration. "Sorry, I'm probably not the best one to ask. Never studied the art of removing stains. Either way, this is just water. To get you started." She handed him the wad of towels.

"Thanks," he said, grabbing the towels with his right hand and accidentally touching hers. The exuberance he felt with that touch was almost enough to balance out the rest of this awful night.

He dabbed the red, wet spot on his pants with the towels to no avail. "Um. The night is pretty much a zero for me, though. I can't go back in there like this." They both silently looked down at his crotch and he felt the heat rise again in his cheeks.

"Ah, Bill Griffin," she said, and he felt his heart burning with the sound of his name coming from those beautiful lips. "There must be some way I can help you make this a better night than it's been so far. There's always hope for improvement, right?" She leaned into his shoulder and Bill hesitated to look at her. What if she was mocking him? What if this was just some kind of high-school prank?

But he did. He looked up and into those incredible hazel eyes again.

"Dance with me." He said it as if he had said it hundreds of times in the course of his life. He held his right hand out for her, still not breaking eye contact.

"Now?" she asked. "Even with your suit—"

"Fu–Screw the suit. Dance with me," he repeated.

She took his hand, and they rose together as if in a dream. This would always be his dream, right here. They climbed the stairs he had just fallen down, and he opened the Grand Hall's door, and in they went.

They commanded full attention. Mean girls, football team, basketball team, student council do-gooders, geeks, and choir nerds, all of them stopped as Bill and Clarity made their way to the dance floor. Poised and perfect in her beauty, Clarity nodded and smiled at them all, as if she were completely confident walking with the one-handed loser with his giant crotch stain.

Everyone stared at the two of them. They stared at *him,* the invisible boy, stunned. It was like the ending of one of those unbelievable ancient after-school vids where everything works out for the underdog. Ball goes whooshing through the hoop in slow-mo, or into the end zone by an inch, and the crowd goes wild for the kid everyone hated just moments ago.

He felt like he would have a heart attack at any instant.

"Um," he managed. "Won't Barkly have a problem with this?"

She turned to him with a perplexed look on her face. "Chad? He doesn't own me, Bill. It's not like he's got me chained up at his beck and call, right? I mean," she said, casting a look around at their gaping audience, "we've been out a few times, but it's not like we're a *thing*, or anything."

He had been grossly misinformed, then. A fire lit in his gut and he took her in his arms just as a slow song started to play.

This was his moment, after all.

The lavender, the silk of her hair, the arms that willingly draped up and over his neck, the heat from her body, the softness of her skin on her back where his right hand rested. Dizzying, blood pumping, moment.

Were they even swaying to the music? Were there any other people in this room? He pulled away from her, knowing he needed to speak.

"Um. You're a really good dancer," he said. *Idiot, idiot, idiot. As if you have anything to compare this to.*

"Well," she said, "That's because I have a good dance partner." Her smile lit up her face, warmed him.

"Really? No, really? I never really thought I could dance at all," he said, just the trace of a stutter emerging.

"Of course not, Bill Griffin. You've been underestimating yourself for as long as we've been in school together. It's probably your biggest life hurdle. Like if your life was a game? Your self-esteem would be your biggest monster to slay."

"Ah, well I guess I just don't like people who brag too much about themselves," he said.

She gazed intently into his eyes, and softly said, "You intrigue me."

Bill almost responded with 'I know'. But he checked himself in time when he remembered her notes again in her journal. Did he need to confess about reading her notebook? Wasn't honesty at the very foundation of any good relationship? *Relationship? This is just a dance, you idiot.* He grimaced at the voices in his head.

"I have a confession to make," he said out loud, but she reached up to his lips with a delicate finger, its tip so beautifully painted red.

"Shhhh," she said. The sadness had returned to her face, and she pulled even closer to him. "I want to enjoy this moment, just as it is. Before I…"

Whatever she was about to say, she had decided that it was better left unsaid for now. Bill didn't want to push it. Instead, he tightened his embrace and closed his eyes. This was as good as life had ever been.

The song started to wind down, and they pulled away to stare at each other again, when Bill realized that Clarity wasn't looking into his eyes anymore. She was looking at his lips.

He stopped thinking. The voice in his head stopped talking.

He leaned in as they both closed their eyes, lips parted.

"Stay off my girl, loser!" Bill felt a brute force on his shoulder as he was violently shoved away from

Clarity, who stumbled backward on her heels. Bill watched her right herself, then let his anger propel him.

"What the hell, man?" He turned toward Chad, who was leaning menacingly in toward him with his hands clenched into fists in front of him.

Bill reached out with both hands to shove Chad away, but Chad grasped onto Bill's prosthetic with a sneer on his face.

And then he wrenched the prosthetic clear off of Bill's arm. The traumatic memories of that day when Bill lost his real left arm came rushing back. Memories that were supposed to remain buried as a protective mechanism by his psyche overwhelmed his rational mind.

Bill promptly passed out.

Chapter 9: Probe

Bill's snoring woke him up, unless there was some monster with him in the room that sounded like his grandfather's old leaf-blower.

As he lay there, a deep sense of longing enveloped his heart. He recalled that last moment with Clarity, their almost-kiss from so many years ago. Damn that Chad. By the time Bill had recovered from his ordeal, Clarity was gone.

Aunt Em had told Bill that Clarity stayed with him the entire time he was out, up to the moment when she had to leave. Unbeknownst to everyone except her parents at the time, the date for her departure for the accelerated program at the Outer Planets Academy had been pushed up. That was probably what Clarity was trying to tell him before they almost kissed.

Shaking his head, Bill became aware of his present surroundings. He tried to sit up, but the metal straps held him fast to the pallet.

Kimra's back was to him, and even though he was still groggy, he took advantage of the moment to study her ass. Correction, to gawk at her perfectly honed ass, which reminded him of Clarity. He wasn't *that* groggy. All tucked in with tin, the foil was creased and flattened so that the lights of the room reflected off her body as if she were a multi-faceted diamond. She seemed to be having a conversation inside her head again, and he could have sworn she chortled. She held his old fucked-up prosthetic in her hand.

"Into the recycling bin, then," she said, and she chucked his very expensive, very old friend of a hand and forearm into a royal blue bin that waited next to her pedestal.

Fuck, that hand. That hand had seen him through some very dark times.

And in his groggy, fogged up state of mind, remembering loading vids, gingerly holding magazines, playing with his own simple but good enough imagination, Bill Griffin shed a tear.

"Funeral for a friend," he mumbled, and Kimra turned around.

"Beg pardon?" she asked.

"Love lies bleeding in my hand." And with that, Bill once again fell asleep or passed out.

It was a weird kind of sleep, though. The kind of stupor an Earthling gets when he's got some kind of head cold and he takes the special green pills that make his dreams seem like video games. He's awake and in control of what happens in the dream, so can he really call it sleep?

In his REM state, Bill saw an oblong, grayish blob floating in mid-air. Kimra was somehow manipulating it from her workstation. The blob was translucent, and Bill could see microcircuits forming within the shapeless apparition. Then the blob took on a more defined shape. At first, multiple stubs protruded from one of the distal ends of the oblong blob. The stubs elongated to look like fingers. Four fingers and a thumb, to be exact. The rest of the blob began shaping up to look like a hand, wrist, and forearm.

Then Bill heard a soft, whirring sound. It took on a hypnotic, rhythmic pace. In his dream-like state, his consciousness drifted off for what seemed like hours.

He opened his eyes just in time to witness Kimra perform the same disappearing act on his clothes that Rikki had earlier, like what, a year or seven ago. Kimra touched him on the chest, and the comfy top and trousers just faded away like sugar on his tongue. Speaking of sugar, Kimra's hair was not black, it was the color of cotton candy. How could he have gotten it so wrong? It was blue or pink or purple, but certainly not black. She looked sweet and he wanted to lick her. Yes, he wanted to taste her freshly spun beauty in all his nakedness.

Naked. He liked to sleep naked. Dreamed of girls watching him walk naked through parking lots, all of them pointing to him and saying, "Ooh, Aah! Look at Bill!" And he would lay them down on the hoods of their cars and show them who was boss. A favorite dream.

But this? Wait, he wasn't dreaming after all. Some drug. Some strange metal half human had ripped off his prosthetic, he'd passed out, and now here he was. Naked again.

No!

Bill still felt the cold alloy of the pallet, chilling his buttocks. And now his shriveled organ was exposed for the universe to see. Or at least for Kimra to see. How humiliating. Did she understand the concept of shrinkage? How was he going to explain it to her? Maybe he didn't have to.

Swallowing his pride, Bill decided to ignore it and hoped that Kimra would too. He kept his eyes cracked open just a teensy bit and watched her.

She maneuvered around him like the science goddess she seemed to be, fluid and beautiful, luminescent and sharp. Holding his stump in her hands, she scanned it with a shiny hand-held gizmo that was attached to the wall with a slinky-like coil. Oh, good. It didn't appear that she took any notice of his shrunken organ.

Instead, she walked over to a glass-hooded cabinet and removed something from within. With Kimra's back to him, he couldn't see what the object was. Until she turned around to face him.

In her hands was a newly printed prosthetic, complete with forearm, wrist, hand, and fingers. It was the same object that Bill had seen in his dream. Perhaps he was half-dreaming and half-watching her as she created this new prosthetic, using what seemed to be a 3D holographic imaging system.

She hummed as she grabbed his stump and fitted the prosthetic over it. All the while she touched him, she hummed. Bill couldn't identify the tune, but it calmed him. Satisfied that the new forearm and hand were secured, Kimra let it go and watched as it flopped down on the pallet beside Bill.

To Bill, the new arm just felt like a dead weight attached to his stump. Try as he might, he couldn't get it to respond in any way. He didn't know he could feel any more vulnerable and exposed until now.

Great! Can't even cover my junk with this junk!

When Kimra turned away again, he spied his trusty old helmet on the floor beside the pallet. Oh, to be free of the restraints! If he could only cover up the one thing that would give up the ghost for him.

Totally ignoring his limp prosthetic among other limp things, Kimra approached the pallet again. Bill felt her fingers between his lips, opening his mouth. She smelled of WD-40, but tasted like warm icicles, if there were such things. Her filament explorer went over his tongue, behind his teeth, and Kimra, whose face was so very close to his, hummed an audible "Ahh."

She moved to the base of the pallet and parted his legs, running the filament explorer from the bottom up, through the crack of his ass. Bill clamped his eyes shut and his heart started to beat faster. As much as he hated to admit it, he was torn. Yes, he was being assaulted on some level, but at the same time, how often does a guy from Earth get this kind of attention from a seriously beautiful, if maybe not fully human, woman?

As he watched, she lit up; the skin on her arms, her foil covering, her necklace, even a band that secured her hair, circuitry pulsing azure blues and magentas and whites, and all the time she hummed. She held her eyes at half-mast.

She moved to his penis, and placed the tip of the filament inside it, and that just did it.

"HEY! What the fuck are you doing?" Bill jerked his head up and widened his eyes at her in terror. He was even more horrified to see that his ridiculous member had chosen this moment to stand at attention.

"Would you like additional sleep, Bill Griffin? If it would make you more comfortable to be in a suspended mental state while the procedure continues, it won't affect the outcome. Please know, though, that I am almost finished with this initial preparatory examination, and I need your neural center of cognitive functions to be completely operational before proceeding with the necessary phage transfer."

"Phage?" Bill couldn't meet her eye, not with her little filament thing sticking into his dick. He stared at the ceiling. "Are you telling me you're turning me into a Borg? Are you taking away my identity?" He cautiously stole a glance at her, but she continued to stare at his crotch. "Um, excuse me? My eyes are up here. Most women I've been naked with have at least kissed me first."

"Most women?" Kimra asked, a pitch-black eyebrow raised. "There have been women? In naked situations such as this?

"Well, fuck, not like *this,* no." He swallowed and there was an uncomfortable silence. "Okay, so *the* woman."

"*The* woman?" Kimra's eyes narrowed.

"Okay. You got me. The woman of my dreams, how's that? You happy now, with this loser of an Earthling virgin splayed out for you to dig around in? That make your job worth waking up for in the morning? Huh?" Ah, anger. At least it brought his beast down to rest.

If the anger hadn't done the trick, Kimra's next tool of the trade surely would have. What had to be the largest fucking needle in all the universe was pointed toward the ceiling, a little bead of liquid begging to get out of its syringe.

"Negative! Fuck! Get that thing away from me! Help! For fuck's sake, Help! Somebody!" Bill cried real tears, not just one, this time, and he flailed as much as he could, given his metal restraints.

I don't want to get fucking Borged!

All flustered and tuckered out from his futile attempt at freeing himself, he wailed, "I don't want to get Borked..." He was too flustered to correct his error, but he was sure Kimra knew what he meant.

Kimra cocked her head and as he howled, Bill watched her partake in another unspoken dialogue. The door opened at the other side of the room, and in walked a blue sea creature. He would have liked to have called her an octopus or a squid, but this creature wasn't slimy or dumb-eyed.

She, and yes, it was definitely a she, walked on the tips of her tentacles, petite and graceful like a dancer in a tutu, except this woman didn't have a tutu on; she wore a white film sheath that had holes in it for several of her bottom tentacles, while those on top just flopped over the sheath. She had no breasts, at least none that Bill could see, but other than the modest material, she wore nothing at all. The tentacles acted as arms and legs.

The alien was nothing Bill could have conjured in any dream before now. Going forward, he knew there would be more than one night filled with wondering just how those tentacles would feel wrapped around his body. Bill thought his mouth was dry until he felt the drool drip off his chin.

Her head was blue, too, and she had no hair, but tuna-can sized, violet eyes, wide and serene. Something in those eyes softened Bill inside, something far away and familiar that made him think maybe this nightmare would actually work out. She looked directly at him and one of those eyes winked at him. She smiled with a very small, pursed beak-like mouth.

But of course, Bill thought grimly. The tentacles. They wrapped around his already restrained body and hugged him so tightly that he could barely breathe. This octo woman lay on top of him and just held him. He inhaled deeply and enjoyed the intimate moment until he felt an excruciating pain when the injection went directly into his scrotum.

"Ahhhh!" yelled Bill. "You shot me in the balls!"

"Do not be like a human infant," said Kimra, massaging the loose, wrinkly skin over the injection point. "Would you have preferred the shot on the arm or buttocks?"

"What? I had a choice?" asked Bill incredulously. "Well, then hell yes. Either arm or butt or both would have been a better choice."

"I chose the injection spot randomly. Had I known—"

"What's happening to me?" interrupted Bill, as he felt his insides react to the shot, like a million microscopic worms invading every crevice and passageway in his body.

The octo creature got up from the pallet, releasing her grip around Bill. He gathered his breath and moaned, "What have you done? Kimra, what in all that's holy did you just do to me?"

"You have been Borked," responded Kimra. She and Octo both smiled down at him as they retracted his restraints.

And when Bill Griffin finally sat up, ready to scream bloody murder, he caught sight of his new prosthetic, which was now flexing its joints at the wrist and fingers. "Well, damn."

Chapter 10: Hand over Hand

While Bill studied his new appendage, he watched his hand light up from beneath the skin. Delicate white lights flashed and rippled together in a kind of symphony. They reminded Bill of the old-fashioned Christmases he'd had at Gram's house, the way they'd string those miniature antique lights all over the Victorian's porch, and then sit on the swing and watch the lake reflect those alabaster flashes.

The new forearm was slightly larger than his real, right forearm, making him look a bit like a lop-sided Popeye. But what the hell. Beggars can't be choosers. Starting from the wrist, a row of circular buttons ran up to a third of his arm. They lit on and off in a pattern of red, orange, blue, green, and yellow.

Am I supposed to press those buttons? What the fuck? I don't even know what they do.

While contemplating why his new arm would have buttons that required pressing with his real hand, Bill wondered if he could return it for a refund.

Then the reality of his situation wafted through his thoughts. With as little obvious self-consciousness as possible, he used his other hand to cover up his crotch. He looked up and smiled at the blue woman when a long blue tentacle retrieved his trusty helmet and placed it nonchalantly over his junk.

"Thank you," he said as he put his hand over the helmet. "And thank you for lying on top of me like that. If I hadn't been so shit-faced scared of that needle, I might have actually enjoyed it a bit more."

"Anytime," she said. "I do not understand how you and the other crew members do with so few appendages." She made the little pursed-lipped beaky smile again. "I am Cali." She reached out with two tentacles and caressed both sides of his face. Her caress was nothing he had ever experienced and not surprisingly, totally erotic and Bill's imagination took off.

He closed his eyes until Kimra cleared her throat, a rumble of a distant snow blower.

"Do you have further inquiry as to your injection, Bill Griffin?"

He tore his eyes away from Cali to glare into Kimra's eyes, which had turned ebony. "Well, let's see. You just shot my balls with something that will allow my new prosthetic to work properly. That much, I know. Anything else I should be aware of?"

"It may take some time, but you have been given limited access to the cluster," responded Kimra.

"What do you mean, limited access to the cluster?" asked Bill.

"Put into terms you will understand, it means we will be able to communicate with you telepathically," said Kimra. "The language center in your brain will also be enhanced, providing you with a built-in universal translator. You will possess the ability to communicate with those who do not speak the same native language as you."

"Oh," said Bill, scratching his head. It was all overwhelming for him. "Any side effects that I might want to look out for?"

"Although rare, other species have reported dizziness, diarrhea, heart palpitations, uncontrollable drooling, insomnia, priapism–"

"Priapism? What's that?" interrupted Bill.

"Put into a less scientific term, it means errant erections. Apologies if my application of English is too intellectual. I will endeavor to use a mid-intellect level when speaking with you," answered Kimra.

Bill should have felt chagrined at the thought of being considered not very intelligent, but he was more concerned about having an erection at the most inopportune moment on a ship full of women. He tried to think of something smart to say but missed his moment.

"Do not be alarmed," Kimra continued as she checked the monitor. "Those side effects have all been reported only after long-term use. At any rate, the injection has already begun its discourse. Your knowledge, learned, instinctual, and reflexive, will now be uploaded to our database, and in turn, that database, filled now with every networked being's cumulative knowledge, will connect back to you. Simultaneously, the mecphages will also be searching for natural talents, skill levels, potentialities, weaknesses, capabilities, and fail states."

Bill felt his eyes glaze over. Maybe a previous numbing drug was still at work, but he needed a nap. Still, Kimra droned on.

"It will interest you to know, or at least it *should* interest you to know," she said, "that the mecphages will also work to repair your body when you are damaged, energize you when you begin to flag with fatigue, and once the mecphages ascertain that your genetic base is malleable, they will give you the ability to access your more dormant genes. Even to level up, so to speak, if that makes it easier for you to follow."

That woke him up. "Level up? You mean—"

"As it pertains to your graduating to a new level of skill. Commencing new challenges, yes. The mecphages will infiltrate your neural pathways so that your physical vessel will fully cooperate with your actual being. As well as with other beings. As you were, your brain was reacting inefficiently in times of stress or damage. It would trigger a hormonal imbalance or mobilize white blood cells within your system to combat infections and open wounds.

"The cells at the site of damage can make a direct request for assistance, bypassing your neural pathways entirely. Your brain can concentrate on what is time crucial while your organs and systems work toward wholistic physical function."

Bill stared at his hand, now lighting up like the old Chrysler building. It looked like Kimra's hand, really. Not silver, but shining with the incandescence of those lights. As he watched, he concentrated on grasping, flexing the perfect fingers, and rotating his wrist. He reached out and touched Cali on what would have been her breast, if she'd had them. She gently removed it with a tentacle and her blue skin flashed a reddish purple, which Bill perceived as a blush.

It was almost too much to think about, and he felt again the need to sleep, to escape the overload.

"Your hand," Kimra said as she watched the exchange, "will slowly but very steadily gain the ability to integrate with the signals dispatched by your neural network. You must be patient in the meantime, as it accumulates information from your memory cells. Soon it will be fully functioning, cooperating with your intentions and desires."

While she spoke, Bill scratched his nose with his new index finger, scraping away a good layer of skin, and leaving a long, bloody mark. Then he tried to get a bit of crust out of his eye, but it was a bit of a miss, and the finger went all the way into the eye instead.

"Fuck! Oh, excuse me, sorry," he said, watching the hand ball up into a fist, then fold over the four fingers so that he could look at his new fingernails.

"Um, Kimra? How careful do I have to be until it's functioning on all eight cylinders?"

"I beg your pardon? I am not familiar with your cylinder talk."

"Oh, sorry. I mean until it's functioning at a hundred percent, should I stay away from handling, I don't know, delicate objects?" While he spoke, it was almost as if the hand had a mind of its own. It reached out to Cali's face and gently plucked a beautiful black eyelash from her cheek.

Kimra made that faraway snow blower sound again. "I believe you and your hand have just answered that particular inquiry."

"How about strength?" he asked. "I'm assuming this will be stronger than, say, my last prosthetic? Stronger than my other hand is?" Again, his new hand reacted on its own. Bill watched wide-eyed as the hand flashed its lights, picked up the helmet that so nicely covered his crotch and with a couple of sickening crunch sounds, squeezed that beloved helmet into pieces. One of the bigger pieces fell back to smack him in the crotch and he howled, more from surprise than pain.

Kimra cocked her head. "I have downloaded vast banks of information regarding male human anatomy and have not understood the fear and angst that accompanies the external male reproductive components, not having witnessed it firsthand until most recently." She blinked and moved her gaze from Bill's crotch to his face. "Would this be considered the *Achilles Heel* per your ancient humans? I have a special file in my databank for that story."

Bill smiled for the first time in what seemed like eons.

"Well, I guess I never thought of it that way. Achilles' heel was weak because his mom had to hold him when she dipped him into the River Styx. She held him by the heel, and that's the only part of him that didn't get wet. So, since my stick hasn't ever gotten wet, either, I guess you could call it my Achilles heel, right?" He laughed, but both women stood before him, blinking.

Now it was his turn to clear his throat. "So, ladies. If we revisit the past hour or so, I would chance to guess that since you have replaced my, um, appendage here with such an extraordinary mechanism, and since I still speak and laugh, that would lead to the conclusion that you mean to keep me around? Not eat me or otherwise seek my demise? Jeez, I'm starting to talk like you, Kimra."

Her brow knitted together, all shiny and flashing, and as she focused on his face while talking, Bill was once again reminded of Clarity, and of sitting in that library so long ago, smelling the books and watching her twirl her red curls between her fingers as she read. He totally missed what Kimra was saying and didn't even notice that his comfy clothes were back and, thus, covering his Achilles heel quite nicely.

"Hm?"

"I said," Kimra emphasized, "How do you feel now, Bill Griffin? A fairly basic question in line with human discourse."

"Well, let's see. Do you refer to physical, mental, spiritual, or emotional *feel*? Because you might get very different answers to all of those segments of me, and frankly, I'm too damn hungry to be able to concentrate enough to give you an answer that would make you think I'm intelligent."

"That is nothing to worry about, Bill Griffin." Kimra smiled to herself. She held her head at a slant and closed her eyes for a moment, and they all heard the sound of the door opening. Rikki nearly floated in, so even and fluid was her gait.

"Sssomething to taste, yes?" she said, and she smiled as she touched his new hand. The yellow of her skin once again mesmerized him, but he nodded.

"Yes, Rikki, that would be great. Even a bug would work, anything." All three women smiled at each other in that conciliatory way women at a playground would, watching their children.

"Rikki, please take Bill Griffin to Surrep, and ask explicitly for human food. He has mentioned pikelets. See if they are in her databank, and if not, we shall research."

"Gosh, Kimra Doc, I mean Doc Kimra," Bill said, extending his right hand for a shake. "I just can't tell you how much I appreciate everything. Well, not everything, obviously, like the ball shot, but you know what I mean. Thank you."

She reached out and shook his hand.

A surge of some long ago or future memory passed between them. Which it was, he couldn't tell, but it was home and it was hope all at once, a warmth and a steely cold together.

While Rikki guided him out of the examination room, Bill craned his neck to keep his gaze on Kimra, even as the silent door closed between them.

Chapter 11: Wiki Elixir

"Isss your sssoul sssurging ssslightly?" Rikki placed a smooth yellow hand on the back of Bill's neck and squeezed.

"Ooh, that's good," Bill said as she massaged and guided him all at once, one-handed. "Wow. But what do you mean, soul surging? And tell me, do you go out of your way to speak with lots of esses in your sentences? To sound more sssnakey?" He smiled at her when her sharp tongue slipped out from her lips. "I mean, not that there's anything wrong with that. I just wondered if it's natural or if you have to concentrate to get those certain syllables out."

"Hm. sssssCertainly not," she said. "I have not noticed. And if I do, that is just the way I sssay thingsss." She steered him to the right, down another hall. The hallways changed décor as they got farther away from the exam room. Now, the floors were black and white with sparkled inlay, and the walls glowed a soft seafoam, then a delicate rose. Very pleasant.

"Tell me," Rikki went on, "What did Kimra have to say about your physical vessel? Do you find your new digits sufficiently surprising?" She ran her hand from where it had cupped his neck down to touch his new hand, and Bill felt every one of her fingers undulate as they traveled down his arm. He refrained from his desire to take those fingers and lick them, one at a time.

"I don't know how to even answer you on that one, yet. It's too new, you know?" Bill shivered when she laced her fingers with his new ones, and his hand's circuitry lit up. "But maybe you can answer one of my questions?"

"I shall try, Bill Griffin."

"Right before you led me out of her exam room? Kimra shook my hand, and it literally rocked my world. Like electric slide crazy. Like I thought maybe something inside me was getting burned and frozen all at the same time."

"Ah," Rikki said. "Do you think you might be in emotional turmoil, what you call love? Is that what you are saying?"

Bill looked sideways at her to see if she was making fun of him, but she was staring straight ahead with those giant reptilian orbs of eyes. Not even a hint of a smile played on her face.

"Um, no. That's definitely not what I was saying. I'm wondering if there's something that maybe got transmitted from Kimra to me, just in that handshake back there."

"I am not qualified to explain the significance of Kimra's methods, Bill." She stopped, and he stopped as well. "Can I call you Bill? Is that too familiar?"

"No, not at all. Of course! It's my name, right?"

Bill felt his cheeks get a little red, and then felt a sudden jolt of cold to replace the heat.

What the hell was that?

He looked into Rikki's curious eyes as they searched his. And he knew, suddenly. He knew the planet that she had come from, and how it was destroyed. He saw her taken captive, saw a recipe for some sort of rodent dish in a database that hadn't been accessed in years, and he knew Rikki had planned to gorge herself later that evening and languish in bed most of the day tomorrow.

"Hey, wait, stop," Bill said. He put his arm out and they faced each other. "I just need a minute to hash this out with someone."

"Hash? Hm, I am familiar with that Earth dish," Rikki said. "You should be able to get hash at Surreptitious, I am almost certain."

"Syrup who?"

"Surreptitious. That is the name of the dining facility."

Bill watched as her tongue flicked in and out of her mouth with every sibilant. "Um. No, when I say, *hash it out*, I mean I need to talk to you or someone about something. Although, yes, eating hash sounds good, too. Can I ask another question?"

"Certainly."

"Just now, I got this full-on scenario in my head about you. Where you're from, some of the things you plan to do, a recipe even."

"Ah. The tendrils of the cluster are starting to take hold then, yes," she said.

"The *cluster*? Oh, got it. Kimra told me that, but what exactly *is* the cluster?"

"Let us seek out seats at Surreptitious, and we can speak more easily there." She took his hand again, and Bill had a flash in his memory? Brain? Dreams? Just the two of them, Rikki slithering all over his body in some strange bed, her lovely pink pointed tongue gently tickling his inner thighs. Bill shuddered.

"What the fuck," he said under his breath. This wasn't exactly a bad thing, what was going on right now, but weird? Definitely weird.

Turned out Surreptitious was like a chromed-out mess deck, run by a creature they called Surrep. Female exotics populated the place, pressing buttons and waiting for less than a minute for food to be presented on sliding trays that came straight out from slots along the walls. Bill watched agog as steaming dishes, whole fish, heaping bowls of greens rolled out to waiting hands that nonchalantly took their trays while they chatted with others.

One gigantic horseshoe of a table ran its length along three of the walls in the room that was the size of a couple fancy hotel lobbies put together. Soft funky electronic music pulsed quietly in the background while the lights along the walls faded in and out to the music's beat.

Rikki touched Bill's elbow and pointed to a woman who was fast approaching them. "This is our beloved Surrep," she said. He looked at Rikki for any trace of sarcasm but saw none.

"Hello, hello, Surrep to Earthling!" said the woman as she came up to them. She went straight in for the hug before Bill knew what was happening. When she held him at arm's length after their hug, his eyes trailed down her chocolate brown hair that was so long she probably had to sweep it out of the way when she sat down.

Surrep wore a purple vest and pink pants; the vest was unbuttoned and wide open. Alarmingly wide open, revealing two, four, six, eight breasts, all lined up like a mother Labrador retriever, all of which flopped around just barely concealed by the vest's two front sides.

"Hell… hell… hello," Bill managed to squeak out as he turned the shade of Surrep's pants. She smiled as his nostrils flared and his head fell back.

The smell of this woman. Bill closed his eyes unabashedly and inhaled as if it were his first breath after being under water for a full minute and a half. She smelled of honeycomb, of jam and biscuits, of sweet cornbread, of Crème Brule, of maple sugar and sugared cinnamon, of every mouthwatering morsel of sweet food he had ever tasted.

He opened his eyes to see both Rikki and Surrep smiling down at him. Yes, this Surrep creature was also tall. Not Rikki tall, but still basketball-player tall, tall enough that her delightful buffet of tantalizing breasts dangled at his eyes' height. The sights and smells made him just want to eat her, literally eat her. He bit his lip and forced his eyes back up to meet hers.

No introductions were really necessary, as that weird tingling came to Bill once again, under his skin and lighting up his hand and bursting in his brain. He knew Kimra's mecphage injection, or maybe that handshake, maybe both were responsible for the instant warmth he absorbed from Surrep. He couldn't see memories or dreams, though. No plans or regrets, either. But a kindness wafted off her and into him that made him want to put his head on any of those eight lovely teats and just weep with pure joy.

He did wonder, though. Something was missing in his connection with Surrep. Maybe it was in just having met her? Something was deliberately being hidden, he thought as he narrowed his eyes and stared into hers. Maybe he just needed time to absorb her.

Surrep took his hand and all thoughts left Bill's head. She ran a finger along his lips and said, "Hmm," then parted his lips and slid an exploratory finger along his teeth, over his whole tongue, and then the roof of his mouth. When she touched his uvula, he gagged, and she jerked away.

"Oh my." Seeing that Bill had stopped gagging, she said, "I am merely testing for your food preferences, Honey."

"Can't you just read me? Or wait, here's a wild idea. *Ask* me?"

"Oh, what fun would that be?" She threw her head back and let forth a full belly laugh, a laugh that he thought sounded like now-extinct Earth itself, loud and unafraid of judgment.

Bill felt aroused, watching her as all eight breasts undulated like bowls of synchronized gelatin. She then touched each one of her breasts and made a slurping, guzzling kind of sound, all the while with a transfixed gaze on his bemused expression.

He was, with no doubt, mesmerized.

The women nodded at each other, some decision having been reached, and Rikki led him with that velvety hand of hers to a table, where she pulled a seat out for him. Bill felt slightly embarrassed by the reverse chivalry of his hosts, or hostesses as they may be, and reluctantly took the seat.

He looked up at Rikki, who had remained standing.

"Aren't you going to join me?" Bill asked.

"Oh, I have many tasks to perform before I can feed. I may have to grab something on the run and hope for the best. Meanwhile, there is much to do before I can indulge," said Rikki.

Confused at her words and at a loss for his own words, Bill just nodded, his mouth opening slightly as if to say something.

"I shall return, Bill," Rikki said. "When you are sufficiently satiated. Salud!" She swayed out of the hall like a 1940s movie star, and Bill watched her perfect yellow ass until it disappeared around the corner.

He waited impatiently as his stomach shouted out to him. Thank the stars this place was loud enough to not give away his borborygmi. He watched with fascination and just a little bit of horror as the women creatures all around him ate and laughed. They kept their distance, though, and several painful memories from his high-school cafeteria rose to the surface. Only this time, he didn't have a comm-screen to hide behind. He tried to look bored.

Surrep finally reappeared, carrying a tray that was stacked seven inches high with the most magnificent pikelets Bill had ever seen. His eyes widened at the tiny pitchers that stood at attention beside the dish, filled with different colored syrups. He dipped his new prosthetic index finger into one of the pitchers for a sampling and brought it to his mouth. The taste of fresh strawberries filled his gastronomic senses. He licked the finger clean, and a smile broke out on his face.

"Surrep, I do believe you are my new hero, I mean heroine," he said, as she made herself comfortable next to him.

She smiled, patting her top two breasts and for a split-second Bill forgot all about the pikelets.

"Go ahead, try them," she nodded. "I will keep you company as I am free of other duties. Fill up, Darling!" She handed him a salmon-colored fork and knife. The fork looked more like a two-pronged spatula, lightweight and flexible. He was reminded of Rikki's tongue.

Holding the fork with his new hand took some getting used to, but he needed to practice. It fell to the plate several times, but Bill persevered, his tongue clenched in his teeth. Finally, he managed to subdue a multi-layered chunk of pikelets with the fork while coordinating cutting them with the knife in his right hand. The hand-off of the fork from left to right hand was less dramatic.

The pikelets were fluffy and warm. He tasted them with all four kinds of syrup. Strawberry, chocolate, maple, and some kind of tropical pineapple-y kiwi concoction, all utterly delightful. They rolled around on his tongue with the precious cakes, warm and sticky, and he washed them down with some incredible thick creamy drink that looked like a fruit-punch flavored convenience store slushee.

"How did you get all this information about my favorite food just by digging around in my gums?" he asked her after swallowing.

"It is my duty, Love." Surrep touched his forearm and his skin beaded up in instant goosebumps.

"So, wherever this ship goes, there will be pikelets?"

"Indeed. Anywhere I go, pikelets go."

"Do all planets have pikelets, I wonder?"

"Well, what does it matter, Sweet Pea? When you have me?"

He stopped talking again to fork in another mouthful of pikelets, thoroughly doused with strawberry syrup. Surrep reached into her vest to pull out one of her breasts. She leaned against him and over his plate and squeezed. When he finally wrenched his eyes away from her succulent chest and back to his plate, his mouth fell open.

There was now whipped cream piled on top of the pikelets.

"How'd you—"

"They are my secret, or maybe my not-so-secret arsenal, Honeybunch. Whatever you want, if it is edible or drinkable, I have it right here." She gave two of her nipples a little pinch.

"Well, now. Astounding," he said, as he dug in again. The pikelets filled a void in his inner body system, like his lifestream finally had something to carry around in there. All of his organs seemed to awaken and stretch in a glorious Sunday morning kind of luxury.

He eyed Surrep as she rested her head in her hand, watching his mouth's every move. Then his eyes traveled down her chest to her abdomen. Such odd protuberances, really, but beautiful, too, and to think they each had stuff inside, just waiting for someone to suck. His eyes closed halfway as he envisioned tasting ice cream, maybe mustard and relish for his hotdog, perhaps French dressing for his salad.

"The possibilities are endless, aren't they?" he asked aloud.

Surrep smiled, and Bill knew what she was going to say before she even parted her lips.

"Indeed." She patted two of her breasts from the bottom and they bobbled a bit.

Bill put the last forkful of pikelets into his mouth, licked his lips, and blinked up into Surrep's smiling eyes.

When he looked up, Rikki was towering over them, alternating her reptilian eyes between Surrep and him.

"Sssorry to disssturb," she said.

"Not at all, not at all," Bill stammered, standing and motioning for Rikki to have a seat. She shook her head and held her hands up, then pointed to the exit.

"The captain wants to sssee you," she said. "Now."

Chapter 12: One in Every Crowd

When Bill first saw the bridge, he was reminded of a scaled down version of the mission control rooms on Earth that were used to launch spaceships. So many workstations and electronics on every wall except the front one, where a large screen served as the focal point. The captain's chair and control console were located prominently in the middle of the chamber, with a couple of seats off to one side that were occupied with women. They could have passed as mannequins in an old-fashioned department store.

Both women had blank expressions and looked like they were completely naked, but like the dolls of way back when, they had no nipples, or any visible female genitalia between their legs. It made Bill want to explore in order to confirm his hypothesis. And to think Aunt Em always said Bill had no innate scientific curiosity. They moved like machines, tilting their necks back and forth while keeping their hands on the workstations. Bill's eyes only rested on them for a heartbeat before moving on to the much more intriguing woman who sat in the command chair.

"Mr. Griffin, I presume," she said, and her eyes darted from his face to his hand in the space of a second. Her flaming red hair hung loose down past her shoulders, parted in the middle and disheveled. She wore a skin suit of green, which nearly matched her skin tone.

He extended his hand out for her to shake but she did that fast hand to eye thing again and chose to ignore the gesture. He awkwardly retracted his hand and cleared his throat.

"Yes" he said, "and I'm guessing you are our captain."

"Well, let us not jump to those conclusions, shall we? I'm the captain of this ship, but I'm not *your* captain, now, am I?" She narrowed her eyes and Bill reflexively pulled his head back, like a turtle in retreat.

"You have been rescued," the captain said, "from an inferior moon that once orbited an inferior planet, and because of that rescue, the *Tenuous Hope* is facing the very real probability of compromise."

"Tssssst," Rikki interrupted, just loud enough for the captain to stop talking. "Thiss iss our captain, Ssanya Rane. She *asked* to sssee you." Rikki let her tongue flip languidly through the air.

As if reminded of her manners, Captain Rane stood and squared her shoulders. She put her hand out and Bill gave it another shot. Their handshake was a terse one, just a single squeeze.

He decided to keep quiet.

She was a pixie of a woman, standing barely five feet tall, with delicate elfin ears that would be seriously sensuous on someone who was not a raging bitch. Every muscle in her body was accentuated by the suit she wore, and all of those muscles were quivering. She reminded him of a cat on a windowsill, just a bit off balance but preparing for the right moment to pounce. She put her hands on her hips and glared up at him, those piercing amber eyes throwing daggers his way from a decidedly off-green face.

"Now, I am not one to cut corners, but I'll be honest enough to tell you that you, the retched corner of that galaxy that was you, was a corner I should have cut. But who am I? I'm just the one following orders. They trust me, and I come through."

"I'm grateful for the rescue, Captain," Bill said quietly, "and very sorry for your inconvenience." Bill was pacing and glancing at the manned, or 'mannequined' stations on the bridge.

"Just stop," she said. "You need not kowtow or patronize me on my bridge, Mr. Griffin. And stop stumbling around before you bump into the TACH console and cause more mayhem."

Bill stopped pacing and glanced toward Rikki in puzzlement. Rikki pointed to one of the consoles on the bridge and mouthed "Tactical Ssstassion."

"What I would ask of you, Earthing, is please keep a low profile while we manage our way out of this sewer system and continue with our mission." Rane jerked her chin toward Rikki and turned as if to take her seat again when the onboard gravitational plane suddenly tilted.

One of the mannequins threw both limbs up to her head and exclaimed, "We have been hit!"

Captain Rane shifted into action mode and bellowed, "Report!"

A crewmember at what Bill deemed to be the engineering station responded, "Inertial dampers are holding steady. The aft shields absorbed the brunt of the hit. No casualties reported."

The captain flew back into her seat. "Battle stations! We have been tracked," she shouted into her console, but her voice was controlled after her first exclamation. "Slippery space sacs! Evasive maneuvers! Now!"

Rane turned back to Bill, did a double take, and barked, "You, Earthling! Get to the crew quarters and stay there. And we can thank your blessed blue home for this attack. Rikki, show him to a bunk and take your station."

Rane was strapping herself in when another gravity shift occurred, but this time Bill felt a noticeable impact. Like hitting a deer in the road, he thought. Or hitting an unexpected lunar rock. The gravitational plane tilted to almost forty-five-degrees, and everyone who wasn't strapped in, the captain included, was thrown to one side of the bridge.

"Captain, helm control is offline. Maneuvering thrusters are non-responsive," announced the TACH crew member.

One of the mannequins, who was working the helm, had been tossed from her seat, hitting a portion of a control panel, and now lay still on the floor. Well, the wall, really.

A flash of gray flew in front of Bill's face, feathery and squawking. Bill reached out with his new hand and grabbed it.

Qeet, his eyes huge and batting, looked at Bill. "Hello to Mr. Bill," he chirruped. There was a moment of peace there, even amidst the rising action and panic. Bill's hand lit up and he felt a surge of energy, and with it came a certainty that somehow this would all work out, this time at least.

After fluttering his wings and squawking a few times at several attempts to teleport, Qeet finally curled around Bill's neck so that his head rested on one of Bill's shoulders.

"What's the matter, little fella?" asked Bill with some concern in his voice. "Why can't you teleport?"

"Qeet upset. Qeet no escape."

Bill felt the creature quivering with fear. "Don't worry, Qeet. I'll keep you safe."

The ship's gravity plane stabilized somewhat but remained askew.

"Ssstep up, now," Rikki said, taking Bill's arm, and motioning toward the exit.

He grabbed onto the safety handles along the wall to steady himself and worked his way toward the door.

Captain Rane turned back toward the command chair, but misjudged the gravity change since the second hit, and lost her balance. She curled herself into a compact green ball as she hurtled toward Bill and he once again reached out with his new hand and grabbed her. Well, he grabbed her ankle.

Held in an awkward way, she repositioned herself until she was completely upside down, facing Bill. Their eyes were inches away from each other's, and

Bill gave her what he hoped would be a chivalrously humble smile.

"Let. Go," Rane growled between clenched teeth.

He wanted to, really. He wanted to let her go and watch her fall, if not with full force because of the gravity situation going on, then at least with a soft bump on her mean head, but at that moment, Bill Griffin was experiencing a full body surge that made all of the muscles in his body spasm.

His eyes flew open wide, his jaw clenched, and saliva filled his mouth. His head fell back and his hand that still held Rane by her Achilles heel lit up like the Fourth of July back home.

It was like a full body orgasm. And he wanted it to go on forever.

The muscles in his arms and legs were contracting, pulsing, and he felt as if he could lift a professional football linebacker back on Earth. Could his muscles actually be growing? On their own?

His mind was calm, as was his breathing. He smiled again as he tipped the captain right-side up and put her down. Her face was a deeper green from anger and too much blood, but she held her tongue.

"Captain, helm control is back online. Maneuvering thrusters working at eighty-five percent," announced TACH.

"Tssst, Captain Rane?" Rikki had taken the helm and manipulated the panels with an experienced calm. "When you are all ssset, and finished testing out our new passenger, we do have certain pressing concernsss."

The captain returned to her chair after shooting another angry look at Bill.

You'd think she'd cut a guy some slack after he just saved her life. Geez.

Chapter 13: Big Blue Violence

"Report!" commanded the captain.

"The source of the attack has been identified and located," said TACH. "The signature of the energy trail matches those of a *Ravager*-class attack ship."

"Hmmm. That's the same type of ship that partook in the attack on Earth," said Captain Rane.

"It isss him, is it not, Captain?" Rikki turned her huge eyes to Rane.

"Bet your asp, it is. Or at least, it's acting under his orders."

"Captain, the *Ravager* appears to be adrift and its engines are offline. Its shields are also down," said TACH.

"Scan the ship and try to access its logs," said Captain Rane.

"It is using an older version of command control that we have previously hacked. It should not be a problem," said TACH.

"Helm, keep our distance. This might be a trap," said Rane, as she kept her eye on the main screen.

"Sensors detect an energy overload within the *Ravager*'s plasma conduits. An explosion is imminent," reported TACH.

"Reverse engines! Now!" commanded Rane. "Brace yourselves!"

Bill felt the ship lurch and watched the main screen as the image of the *Ravager* shrank in the distance. The screen then brightened in a blinding flash. Bill grabbed the deck railing just moments before the ship shook from the oncoming shockwave emanating from the explosion of the *Ravager* attack vessel.

After the *Tenuous Hope's* inertial dampers stabilized and the crew reported minor injuries, attention on the bridge focused on what had just happened.

"Captain. Engineering reports a problem with the main engines. The ship cannot sustain performance above fifty percent for more than six hours at this time," reported Rikki.

Captain Rane released a long sigh and asked, "What else is there to report?"

"We intercepted an encrypted long-range message from the *Ravager* just before it was destroyed. We've also completed the analysis of the *Ravager*'s most recent log entries," said TACH.

"Let's hear it," said Rane.

"The *Ravager* was damaged during the attack on Earth. The power used in the attack was overly excessive and the blowback damaged or destroyed a number of the attacking fleet's ships. This particular

Ravager was to complete repairs and join the rest of the fleet at a pre-determined rendezvous point. When it detected the *Tenuous Hope*, it used most of its remaining power for the attack on our ship, with just enough power left over for its escape.

"The *Ravager* commander didn't expect its engines to fail. It's not clear whether this was a suicide attack, but its safety protocols were disabled, and powering up their disabled engines resulted in an overload of the plasma conduits and the subsequent explosion," reported TACH. The tactical console emitted a short beep. "The last message that was intercepted from the *Ravager* has now been decrypted."

"Put it on screen," said Rane.

The main screen changed from the star speckled blackness of space to the smoky bridge of the *Ravager*. On the screen appeared a male humanoid with the same green skin as Captain Rane. He wore a military uniform but appeared bedraggled, green blood seeping out of the corner of his mouth. In the background, Bill could see that the bridge was in a state of disarray.

"This is Captain Canard of the *Pincer II*. We've encountered an enemy vessel before we were able to complete essential repairs to the plasma drive. My ship is operating under impulse drive only. We were able to attack the enemy and determine its identity as the *Tenuous Hope*. The extent of her damage is unknown.

"It is with much regret that I inform you that my crew and I will not be attending your cause at the rendezvous point. We shall take this last opportunity to annihilate the enemy.

"May you propagate and prosper, oh Great Blue Eminence."

The main screen went blank and then switched back to the star-speckled blackness of the space vista.

Sanya Rane turned to Bill and glared at him. "It is Blue Balzar. The asshole renegade who beat us to that hellhole called Earth, destroyed it and its unnecessary accessory of a moon, and now here he is, making house calls right at our front door." She gave her hair a toss and Bill darted a questioning look to Qeet.

"I'm sorry? And this is my fault?" He felt the anger grow inside him. "Look, lady, I know you're a big important *Captain* and all, but that *hellhole* you keep dissing is, I mean, *was* my home. Everyone I ever loved is *dead* as of yesterday. I'll thank you to—"

"Mr. Griffin? You can thank me later when I'm not worrying about my ship's damage and my crew's safety. Rikki, take him and that obnoxious furred stowaway down to their male quarters. Please. We shall take the *Hope* to Toriff. Damage needs attention, like now."

"Toriff? TORIFF? No, to Toriff?" Qeet had stiffened and clung to Bill's neck with his jagged little claws. He dove headfirst down the length of Bill's body, squeezed into his pants, and scrabbled between his legs until he had a painful grip on parts Bill hadn't thought about since Kimra had manhandled them with her special tools.

Even as Bill sounded a loud and fearful protest, Rikki led him down the ramp toward the exit. Bill walked like he had back in elementary school when he had broken one of his legs. He stiff legged his way for a few steps, then stopped and dug into his pants and carefully dislodged the panicked Qeet.

"What's your problem here?" he asked.

Rikki grabbed Bill's arm, still trying to get them to the door. "Qeet scared of sphere Toriff, ship destination."

"Well, I'm scared of all of you, truth be told," Bill answered, then raised his voice to make sure Sanya Rane could hear him as the door closed. "But since what doesn't kill us makes us stronger, maybe we could all just ease up and cut each other a little slack around here." He huffed a bit and thought he saw a twitch of a smile on Rikki's skinny little snake lips.

Chapter 14: Everybody Has a Dream

They stood at a window and watched, just the two guys, Bill Griffin and Qeet, as most of the crew disembarked, piling personal belongings and excursion bags from the ship and into waiting vehicles on the planet Toriff.

Captain Rane had granted a much-deserved furlough to her exhausted crew. Only she with a token repair crew would remain behind. The ship would be out of commission while the main drive was offline for essential repairs and maintenance. The cooling system and manifolds were at fault and would need to either be overhauled or replaced, depending on the location and extent of the damage.

Bill and Qeet watched Rikki, yellow and brown and impossibly tall, undulating down the ramp and along the pathway outside. Exquisite ass, and all-around majestic physique. Her smooth movements were sensual, like an intimate dance. Bill couldn't place it, but something about the way she held herself seemed familiar, reminding him of Earth.

Then he noted the many others he had yet to meet, winged and gilled and furry, in varied colors and sizes. Bill spotted Kimra, metallic and marching, staring straight ahead, and behind her the woman who wowed him with her warm smells and tastes, Surrep.

Qeet held on from behind, with just his blue feathery head peeking out over Bill's shoulder. The rest of his body clung onto Bill's back.

Apparently, if one had a mechanical issue or battle-related damage in this particular corner of space, Toriff was your best bet as far as trustworthy labor went. They docked at the city of Troit, land of all things transport, from used or new sales to detailing and repair.

Troit spread out flat and uninspiring, its buildings huddled together in a stew of beige and gray. Gravity on Toriff was less than Earth's but more than the old Earth's moon, and there was a chemical compound in its atmosphere that was poisonous to human lungs.

Bill had been instructed to wait on the *Hope* until Rikki or someone could find him an appropriate suit. Rikki apologized in advance, telling Bill it might take a while, since human males in these parts were anomalies, and there was every possibility that a suit for him would have to be custom manufactured. He might just have to stay on board until the ship was repaired.

Bill felt a tinge of depression sink in as he watched Captain Rane see the last of the crew disappear through the gate of the space port. Her green skin turned just a tad yellow out there. She walked with a strut of sorts, and her hands were held stiffly, almost as if she were prepping for a salute. Then she returned to the *Tenuous Hope*, disappearing into the bowels of the ship, to oversee the repairs.

Bill thought back to the last time he had seen people who mattered. The last time he saw his Aunt Emily, she was waving sadly from the porch with a handkerchief. It was supposed to have been a joke of sorts; she had wanted to reenact the olden days, when people would wave from the dock to laden ships bound for what the masses once thought was the other side of the world. But the joke had missed its mark for Bill as he gave his final answer of a wave back to her. He knew he might never see her again.

And of course, he had been right.

Likewise, for his few friends, game boys who had become gaming men, warming their parents' couches and working at dead-end Earth jobs to keep things safe and same.

All dead.

All dead except perhaps for his Clarity, the only one outside his family and inner circle of friends who really mattered to him. It was his hope that she was nowhere close to Earth when it was destroyed. Perhaps she was a safe distance away, still working in the asteroid belt and totally unaware of her home planet's demise.

But whenever he thought of Earth, he thought of her. Now he realized life was indeed fragile, and even though he couldn't truthfully say that these women who had scooped him up from the surface of the moon were friends in any sense of the word, they were the only beings alive who had shared words with him. And for that he was thankful.

Sadly, he reached up onto his shoulder and patted the only creature left to him.

Qeet chirped softly into Bill's ear.

"You going to fill me in on why this place freaks you out, Qeet?"

Qeet pulled himself up a little and snuggled in under Bill's neck.

"Something you'd rather not discuss?" Bill tried again.

"Troiters," Qeet said, "hungry beasts."

"You think they want to eat you?"

"Not think, know, yes. In Troit? Qeet pikelet." He trembled and tucked himself in more. Bill started to walk, to get away from the window and the view that was making both of them sad and afraid.

"You are like a pikelet to the Troiters? Tell me," Bill said.

"Day one," said Qeet, "Qeet ship land here Toriff. Trade things with Troiters. One Qeet like me Qeet but not me traded. All Qeets have same name Qeet. Funny. But this Qeet, she run away on Toriff, in Troit. Hide. And little Troiters find her. Tie her up. Laughing. Then," Qeet stopped and hid his head in his clawed hands.

"That's okay, Qeet, you don't have to tell me the whole story if it scares you."

"No. Qeet here anyway. Troiters tear Qeet arms off. She screeching, crying. Then Qeet legs, too. Rip all off. Beasts eat arms, legs. Qeet still alive, watches."

Qeet made a choking sound and fell forward. Bill caught him with his new hand and they both took big breaths when it lit up.

"How do you know this happened for real, Qeet?" Bill asked, continuing to walk.

"Qeet in trader ship saw. All happen like that. Trap on ship, no teleport because fear."

"Wait, it's not just you? No Qeet can teleport when they're afraid?"

"No. System failure. Always happen." Qeet rubbed his eyes and hid his face in Bill's chest.

Bill felt the little creature, now white like Bill's suit, quivering from his fears in retelling the horrific story.

"Well, now," he said, "as long as old Bill Griffin is around, you know you're safe, little guy." He patted Qeet, but it was more of an awkward swat.

"That Qeet dream."

"What?"

"Qeet dream safe."

Bill smiled down at him. "That's your *dream*? Of being safe? Really?"

"Too much?" Qeet asked.

"No, not at all. And I might just be the one who can make your dream come true, little guy." And just then, so many of Bill's doubts and fears slipped away. He had already survived what he imagined was the most horrific times of his life. Barkly ripping off his prosthetic at the Grad Ball, Earth and life as he knew, gone in a green haze of alien annihilation, and what he had imagined were his final moments on the moon. Yet still Bill breathed.

There was little left to lose. What previous purpose Bill surmised life held for him was for naught in this new existence. Fear had no place and Bill was ready to champion his new creature friend in any way he could.

"Bill Griffin?"

"Yes, Qeet."

"Bill Griffin dream?" Qeet's huge eyes drifted at half-mast now, and his voice became softer.

Bill had to swallow. Suddenly he realized that every dream he had ever had, and every dream that had yet to bubble to the surface, had died with Earth's demise. He had dreamed of climbing Mount Everest the manly way with real rope and surviving only on supplies he could carry on his back, like they did back in the day, without augmented equipment.

And ultimately, perhaps absurdly, he had of course had the dream of Clarity. Being with her, kissing her, smelling her again, watching her as she concentrated over a book or maybe even a griddle. Watching late-night vids with popcorn and sleeping in before sharing pikelets the next day.

And now? Did she even exist anymore? And without a common home, what were his chances, even if she still breathed, of ever seeing her again?

Could *that* be the dream? Just seeing Clarity or knowing she, too, was still alive?

"Bill Griffin?" Qeet's voice was just a whisper now.

"Huh? Oh, yeah, dreams. Well, I guess I need to get back to that drawing board, as they say, Qeet. I guess I might want to track down a character named Blue Balzar, maybe kick his ass around a bit for destroying my beautiful planet. I guess that could be a dream, right?"

Qeet's eyes suddenly sprung open. "That *everybody* dream."

"Yeah? Pretty bad guy?"

"He hurt many. Make bad crew. Bully everybody. Pick dream Qeet can handle."

"Okay, here's a dream. I'd like to see the *Tenuous Hope,* now that we're allowed to move about the ship freely. You can help make that dream happen?"

Qeet sat up in Bill's arms and gave a little furry smile. "Qeet say yes. Good dream. Mr. Bill no dream pretty crew members?"

"Huh?" Bill felt his face turn red. "Do I dream about the pretty crew members?" Was he that obvious, even to this little critter?

Qeet seemed to get even more excited and said, "Qeet can help that too. Qeet know every female on ship."

"Ah. Well, hey now. Why didn't I think of that? Shit, man! Now Bill Griffin has three dreams! We should start writing them down!"

"First, Qeet point, then Mr. Bill walk. We learn Blue Balzar, we learn *Hope*, we learn female. Qeet show, not tell. Words big, Qeet small." He pointed down the hall to their left, and Bill started walking.

The ship was deathly quiet. They walked through corridors and sections, Bill opening doors by touching the sides of walls where Qeet instructed, and neither spoke. Finally, Qeet pointed to a threshold and they entered a room that reminded Bill of the now defunct grand theaters his grandmother used to talk about. It was circular, but instead of the screen being overhead, there was just a simple stage in the center. C-shaped benches rimmed the stage, ten deep.

"Hmm. How do people see over the heads of all those people in front of them? Seems like a stupid setup," Bill said.

But Qeet had vanished. Bill even checked in his pants, but no. He sighed and sat on one of the benches.

Without warning, the lights dimmed, and the stage came alive with music, like an intro to a show, an overture. A flock of what looked like ninja assassin birds chattered as it flew toward Bill. Bill ducked down, raising his arms to protect his head before he realized the advancing aves were just holographic images.

"Be no afraid, Bill Griffin," said Qeet excitedly, as he fluttered in and amongst the avian images to show that they were harmless.

"What is this room?" asked Bill in wonderment.

"K-torium," squawked Qeet.

"K-torium?" repeated Bill. "K as in Knowledge? Like a Knowledge Auditorium?" He gave the chamber another once over and said, "Cool! K-torium. This sounds just like a Wiki room."

"K-torium houses Wicki room, yes!" squealed Qeet. "Bill Griffin understands. *Ask Reeves!*"

"Don't you mean *Ask Jeeves*, little guy," responded Bill.

"No no no, *Ask Reeves!*" insisted Qeet.

"Okay, sure, whatever you say," said Bill. "Show me what you got."

As if on cue, the flock of ninja birds dispersed, and the music faded. Bill watched as pages appeared as they would on any of his tablet screens. A booming, yet sensually soothing, and more than vaguely familiar not quite male and not quite female voice provided the narrative.

Blue Balzar, also known as BB, is revered by his misguided followers, who address him as Great Blue Eminence. Currently, he is the leader of a rogue sect of rebels, a clandestine interstellar group within the organization known as Entropic Dystrophy (ED).

Although not confirmed, rumors abound of BB's origins from the modest town of Mosington, Virginia, United States of America, Earth. Uploaded footage claims to show Blue Balzar as a teenager playing for a junior American football team, the Mosington Warriors.

The words were there, on the stage screen, but Bill was entranced with a life-sized three-dimensional rendering of Blue Balzar himself, elevated so that even if there were audience members ten rows back, they could see him.

Balzar moved like a body builder, changing his poses and facial expressions, most of which were some form of anger. He walked above Bill's head, then squatted right in front of him. The man was large, as far as Earth men go, that is, and indeed he was actually blue. Like hyper-link blue. Bill could almost feel Balzar's phantom breath on his face.

For obvious reasons, Bill was confused.

First and foremost, why on Earth did the presentation have references to Bill Griffin's high school and hometown of Mosington, Virginia? Tentatively, he reached up through the hologram of Balzar and touched the name of his favorite Earth town. Instantly, he was taken to the middle of a street he had walked every day, the street that lead to school. Lined with towering sycamores with great swaths of peeled bark, the street was dappled with sunlight, real light. Bill held his breath as the moving exhibit took him to his high school's front doors.

"Ah," he said under his breath as the scene panned past the wide hall, through the outdated cafeteria with button-tech food displays. He could almost smell the fried potatoes, salted and greased.

So, this Blue Balzar character was from Earth, and was also the one responsible for destroying Bill's home planet. How could that even be? The guy was *blue,* so obviously there was some sort of mistake. He had to be from another planet in another system or from a parallel universe. Maybe Qeet was just playing around, mixing up these entries that looked kind of nebulous to begin with. Maybe Qeet just wanted to show Bill something fun to do while the crew of the *Hope* was elsewhere.

Maybe this was a video game.

And if not, something just had to be done. Bill never worried much over getting revenge for unfair treatment, and heaven knew he had experienced his share of abuse at the hands of the bullies, but now the bile was making a regular, pulsing surge up the back of his throat.

Everything. Everyone. The scientists and poets, the babies and cocker spaniels, and the dairy mart and movie theatres were all gone. He watched the hologram depiction of his school with the mean kids who had yanked his briefs up into his butt crack. Everything was gone.

The moment Bill stood, the Blue Balzar images and the words on the screens disappeared. He gave his head a shake and Qeet appeared, his color fading from blue to beige as he flew up to Bill's shoulder.

"What the fuck, Qeet?"

"What the fuck, Qeet?" Qeet repeated.

"So, this Blue man. He's the dude who just beat us up out there, right?"

"Right, Bill Griffin."

"And he's also the dude who destroyed Earth?"

"We think right, Bill Griffin."

"And for some reason, we think he's from *my hometown*?"

"Not sure, Sir Bill. But *Ask Reeves* not wrong. Qeet help Captain Rane study Earth knowledge to help the Lord."

"Really? I would never had taken the captain for the religious type. But right now, here's what's next, Qeet, my little fuzzy friend. Bill Griffin needs some energizing grub to ponder all this new information. Can you show me where I can find food? Can you get me back to the land of Surrep?" His stomach did a little lurch, and he couldn't tell for sure if it was because of hunger or maybe just the delicious memory of eight perky breasts.

"No, Surreptitious closed. But no worry." Qeet pointed and stood erect on Bill's shoulder as he took charge again. He pointed with his fluffy wing-arm, and the two of them left the K-torium.

Chapter 15: Soft Kitty

Qeet led them into an alcove off the main corridor. Bill guessed it was a storage closet of some sort, but it had nothing in it. Maybe the size of a middle-class Earth kitchen, its walls were lined with inscribed tiles, but the inscriptions were iconographic rather than linguistic. Pictures of sandwiches, drinks, cookies, hot meals depicted with steam lines sprouting from what Bill thought was meat and potatoes, even…

"Pikelets! Holy shit, who would have thunk it, Qeet?" Bill helped the little guy down to the ground and noticed a handy stepping stool he could use to reach up high enough to touch the pikelet icon. The stool was oddly shaped, in that it had a curved surface rather than a solid flat step, and it had seams equally spaced in circular fashion, like overlapping plates. Bill lifted his foot just as Qeet went berserk.

"No stair! No stool!" He flew up into Bill's face and flapped his crazy little triangular arms.

But it was too late. Bill's foot landed on the step and brown fur flew everywhere. In a blast of confusion, he was thrown against a wall before being tackled by a bundle of scratching, hissing fur. He felt his upper arms being punctured just as he hit his head on the floor. Whatever was on top of him was making a low, threatening feline kind of sound, the sound he used to hear beneath his aunt's open windows at night, right before her cat would start a fight. Or a fuck.

He froze and started apologizing, hoping his mecphage-enhanced universal translator was accurately translating his apologies to this crazed creature.

"Sorry, sorry, sorry, please don't hurt me," he said, over and over again.

While he spoke, his hands were clasping this thing around its middle, and he realized that despite the alarming situation, he still had that little portion of his brain that screamed, *Oh, my God, this is the softest thing I've ever felt, ever!*

Its fur was like the rabbit-covered earmuffs the girls used to wear on Earth when it got cold. Only shorter and so much better. Soft, so soft.

After a moment of actually petting this attacker, he came to his senses.

"Hey! I apologized. I didn't mean to use you as a stepstool. Chances are we aren't natural enemies. Hello?"

The claws that had been embedded in his arms slowing retracted, and whatever it was allowed Bill to flip it off of his body. They both stood, and Bill looked down to Qeet, who was covering his mouth with one of his strange little hands.

"Are you laughing at this? Really?" Bill reached down to pick up Qeet, but the brown furball intercepted his prosthetic arm.

Against his will, Bill found his hand buried in that gorgeous stuff, petting it, his mouth dry and his eyes wide. The thing was making a low purring noise now, and it pulled closer to him before he even got the chance to look at it. Suddenly he realized it was licking his hair and nuzzling his neck, all the while sending goosebumps down his body.

"Holy fuck," he said. He finally opened his eyes and gently tried to push the beast away. "Hey, let's get acquainted first, okay?"

He pushed the creature out to arm's length to study it, but it held onto his prosthetic hand, massaging it. The furry beast had enormous luminous yellow eyes and long pointed ears that had tufts of black fur on the tips. Its body was covered lightly with sable downy fur, as was one side of its tail. The other side, the stepstool topside, was like a bendable armor, hard and almost metallic. It made subtle clicking sounds as it curled first up to the body, then unfurled to the floor.

The tail had to have been five feet long, and poofed wide like a beaver's, like a soft paddle, before folding on itself so only softness showed. The creature was on all fours, but now rose to stand on its hind legs, or what Bill thought was hind legs because they looked like normal gorgeous lady gams to him.

Bill did a double take when the creature stood up and he noticed her stunning female features with soft curves at every possible perfect place. He took an involuntary, deep gulp and hoped he wasn't noticeably drooling.

"I am Nialme," she said, in a velvety feline voice. Her tongue, lined with teeny delicate barbs, came out to smooth down some ruffled fur.

"Well, Nialme, nice to meet you. I'm Bill."

"Bill Griffin!" said Qeet.

Bill laughed and shook his prosthetic hand that she was still holding, attempting to mimic a handshake.

"And this?" Nialme looked down at the hand. "What is the name of this?"

Bill looked at the hand in confusion. "Um, this is a hand that I've had replaced."

"Well, this one should have a name, because it made me very excited just now." Nialme's eyes did the slowest blink Bill had ever seen.

Confused and flustered, he asked, "I'm assuming by your obvious anatomy you are one-hundred percent female?" He realized how stupid he sounded as soon as the words came out. *Dork!*

"And I am assuming that it does not matter?" Nialme asked, taking his hand. "We must name this beauty right away, yes?" She took hold of it and casually ran it up and down her brown and black torso. Bill shuddered.

"Name? For my prosthetic?"

"Why not?" she said, and, still holding it in both of her fur-covered hands or paws, she guided it around her body until it clasped her perfect down-covered ass.

Bill closed his eyes and held his breath. This was the stuff of all middle-school dreams. "I, um. I named the other one, actually. It, um, made more sense."

"Yes?" She touched his closed eyes with a soft fingerling. "But not for this thing of wonder?"

"Well, actually," Bill said, getting a grip and opening his eyes, "this one is brand new. I had an accident of sorts on the moon, see, and I—"

"Ah, this is the work of our own Kimra, then?" She pulled herself in closer and before Bill could react, she had flipped him over onto his back and was lying on top of him, his new hand still firmly grasping her furry firm butt.

"Wow, wow," he stuttered. "Yes, Kimra replaced my beat-up one. It lights up at weird times."

"But still no name. What was the name of the other one?" She leaned over and let his real hand reach up to touch her soft brown shoulder.

"Oh, ha, that was from middle school. I named it Andy. You know, stupid rhyme, Handy Andy, get it?"

"It was the one that, shall we say, *performed* best for you, then?" Nialme leaned down over him and once again licked his hair. For a horrible moment, Bill thought maybe he was wetting his pants, because suddenly there was something warm encasing his crotch. When he lifted his head, he saw her tail had splayed and curled underneath him, and now that tail was doing a crazy massage between both of their legs. He gulped again and tried to remember the question.

"Ha, yes, the prosthetic back on Earth was really just there for looks. I mean, the fingers worked, well, at least two of them did, don't get me wrong. Then the Lunar Maintenance Service loaned me one with all five working fingers. It was necessary for the job. But, but..." He started rambling, whispering his words, breathing too hard, wondering about his breath, when he noticed Qeet, who had landed on Nialme's back and was hunched over them, a concerned look in his eyes.

Then in an instant after a flutter of his wings and a squawk, Qeet was gone, disappearing into the air, only to show up again between their chests. He uttered a different high-pitched squawk, trying to keep from getting crushed.

"Is okay? Nialme not hurting Bill Griffin?" Again, Qeet did his teleport thing and appeared at Bill's side, head cocked.

"Qeet. All is well, little cumbersome flit," Nialme purred.

Bill got hold of himself and took her by the shoulders. Gently turning both of their bodies, he managed to stand and again hold her at arm's length before dropping his hands.

"Tasty, Bill," said Nialme. "Is there any way I can help you?"

"Um." Bill forced himself to keep his eyes open. "Actually, I almost used you as a stepstool, see, to reach that." He pointed with his other hand at the pikelet icon on the wall.

Nialme smiled indulgently. "Such a small thing, when you could have asked for something far more satisfying," she said.

She leapt in the air just like a regular housecat would, flying to the top of the wall to gently touch the icon, and when the wall opened and popped out a tray of piping hot pikelets with a little white dispenser full of maple syrup. She grabbed it and landed expertly on her feet. When she handed Bill the full tray, he was surprised to see that no items had shifted or spilled.

His face lit up with a smile at the sight of his favorite meal, but then his eyes searched the room for a place to sit.

Taking his new hand and wrapping it around her shoulder, Nialme said, "We can walk and eat at the same time, yes?" And she tore off a bite-sized piece of pikelet, dipped it gingerly in the syrup, and oh so carefully slipped it between his waiting lips. Then she took a morsel for herself, and after placing it in her mouth, her tongue darted out and licked the top of her nose. Bill gasped in surprise and nearly choked.

"Shall we explore?" she asked.

"Oh, yes," Bill mumbled, still chewing on the bite of pikelet. "We shall. Ahem… explore."

Chapter 16: Interruptus

They linked arms while walking and feasting on the sticky pikelets, all three of them, Bill, Nialme, and Qeet, patting each other once in a while, and Qeet chirruping as he teleported back and forth from her shoulder to his. Bill carried the tray while Nialme fed him the sweet pieces. He watched in fascination as Nialme's tongue swiftly swiped the droplets of sweet, sticky syrup from her lips and nose.

They ended up in the comfort chamber so they could wash off the sticky syrup. Nialme stopped at the entrance with raised paws and hissed at the water coming through the hydra tube.

"What is it?" Bill asked her, drying his hands off on her shoulders.

She lifted her lips to show tiny triangles of teeth. "What is this place?" she asked.

"It's a comfort chamber, you know, a bathroom, see? These are the tubes where we can put our hands to wash them. It's just water! And here," Bill went toward the shower stall, "is where we can wash our whole bodies! We, well, I, would just take off my clothes and jump under this warm clean water. We, or I, would soap up, and rinse off, and we, I mean I, would be clean as new!"

"On my home, there are mountains of sand, none of this water," she said, her eyes magnetized by the water drops coming out of the shower head. "It is very cold and dark and dry. We use our tongues to clean ourselves and each other. You know, in case there are places on us we cannot reach on our own." She smiled and looked at him through unbelievably long eyelashes.

Qeet flew off of Bill's shoulder to land in a pool of water at his feet and gave a happy little chitter. Bill smiled indulgently at both of his new friends.

"You guys make being far away from home, a home that's no longer even there, a lot less lonely and sad, you know that?" He watched as Nialme joined Qeet in the shower. She had wrapped herself up into a ball, like when he had first seen her, and she rolled around under the spray of the shower, Qeet jumping on top of her and running like a lumberjack on a log. She unrolled herself and took Qeet in her paw hands to give him a long, barbed lick from crotch to neck. Qeet chirped in surprise and actually turned a shade of pink.

"Come, Bill Griffin!" Qeet tweeted. "Shower now, get clean!"

Bill looked at his fingernails. They were pretty bad. It had been too long since he had actually soaped up his whole body. Heaven knew what his balls smelled like these days. He hesitated, but as he watched the other two rolling around so unselfconsciously, he threw caution to the wind and stripped down, careful to fold everything as he went.

When he was finally naked, his new friends stopped their waterplay long enough to size him up, so to speak. Bill stood sideways to scooch into the shower, trying to look calm and confident as he picked up a soap tube.

But he kept one hand over his junk, much to Nialme's dismay.

"I say, Bill," Nialme said, "You must relax and not be timid. We are shipmates. We are not biters."

She reached out and removed Bill's hand from his crotch. Both Qeet and Nialme stared at him for what seemed way too long, and to his horror, he started to respond. Nialme smiled and unrolled herself. She turned her back to him and said, "Wash me?"

Still feeling awkward, but definitely enjoying himself, Bill slowly soaped up her back, her beautiful fur now a soft, wet blanket over her back. He rubbed the soap all over her ass, slipping his fingers into its delicate seam.

"I know now what would be a knackname for the Kimra hand, Bill," she said, her tongue playfully catching drops of warm water.

"A nickname, you mean?" Bill's voice came out gravelly at first, then took an awkward climb, cracking almost like when he was a teenager.

"Nickname, knackname, yes. I think your magic hand should be BG. We say BeeGee. You know, your initiatives."

"My initials, you mean?"

"Initials, initiatives, yes. BG. Could stand for Bill Griffin, BIG, Best Gun, Big Guy. Baked Goods. Whatever. You like BG?"

Whether he liked it or not, the hand certainly did. It lit up as it never had, buried in Nialme's wet fur, orange and blue lights with sudden flashes of red. It was when the red flashes turned to a solid ray of light that he heard the voice. It sounded like it was coming from the ship's corridor. Bill turned the shower off and immediately the other two protested.

"Shhh!" he said, his finger to his lips.

And then he heard it again.

"Danger, Bill Griffin."

The voice was robotic and tinny, and it repeated itself now, only louder.

"Danger, Bill Griffin."

Bill didn't even bother to rinse off. If some disembodied voice was warning him about danger, he was going to believe it whether he understood its origin or not. He started putting his skin suit on over his wet body, and nearly tripped over his pants onto the slippery tile. Nialme immediately dropped to the shower floor and made like an over-sided cannonball.

"Intruders on board. Danger. Danger." Again, the weird voice, faraway yet very distinct.

Qeet pounded on Nialme's quivering rolled-up body. "Let Qeet in!" he squawked, knocking on her curved plates. "No eat Qeet! Qeet flee, hide!"

Bill didn't wait to find out if Qeet got to a secure hiding place. Since they had been exploring while eating their pikelets, he had become acquainted with the main layout of the ship. He sprinted across the corridor from the comfort chamber and up three doors.

For the first time since coming on board, his new hand allowed him to gain entry into off-corridor spaces, and he pressed the spots Qeet had shown him. He located a storage room that he had noticed earlier. The door slid open with a swoosh, and he raced back to the comfort chamber, slipping on the soapy floor.

"Nialme, roll this way, hurry!"

Her body in its ball form looked like the old pangolins back on Earth. Some distant flash of high-school biology came to him then, and for an instant he thought of armadillos and caracals and koalas and pythons and bobcats and all the beautiful creatures that had simply ceased to exist just days before. Eons ago, it felt. But then, the voice came booming through the corridors again.

"Danger. Intruders."

"Follow me, Nialme!" Bill took off down the hallway, Nialme rolling along behind him, a noticeable lump in one portion of the perfect ball that he hoped was Qeet, tucked safely inside. They got to the storage room, where the large built-in bins were enclosed and secured. He opened one and lifted the ball of his friends and spoke softly.

"I'm putting you inside one of the storage containers. Stay in a ball, Nialme. I'm covering you with towels. You'll be safe. I'll come back for you. I promise."

"Nrrrp!" A most convincing Qeet sound came from inside the ball, and Bill envied his chirpy friend for a moment.

A surge of information flooded his head as he secured the bin: numbers and blueprints and codes and control diagrams.

"Nrrp!" Qeet repeated, interrupting Bill's revelation of incoming information. His prosthetic hand was alive with color and the imagined sounds of very quiet bells.

"The ship and my hand will keep me safe, Qeet, no worries. I got this."

With confidence he had rarely felt anywhere on Earth and certainly not on the moon, Bill Griffin closed the door of the storage room and ran in the direction that both the ship and his hand were steering him. Right toward the danger.

Where in hell was Captain Rane?

Chapter 17: Vitamin K

Amid the confusion of the ship's very verbal and robotic alarms, Bill Griffin remained uncharacteristically, beautifully calm. All those years tackling video missions and fighting bad guys on Earth had prepared him for this. His breath came in deep, relaxing waves and his mind was focused. It was as if he was in one of his online games.

He ran with ease, in wonder at his muscles cooperating together, so unlike the pathetic days of high-school gym class or his sad attempts at cross-country running. He glanced at his new hand, his BG, and he felt invincible.

"Guide me," he whispered. Whether the strange voice was that of a god, or his own consciousness, he didn't know to whom he was speaking, but it felt as natural as it had when he was just a little boy, playing alone in the woods and pretending he had comrades.

"You need to land softer on your feet as you run." The voice came whispering over his head, still from what seemed like the walls of the ship. Bill looked around to no avail. Maybe it was the same robotic source as the initial alarm, but it was definitely more subdued now.

Bill felt a pang of frustration as he tried to concentrate on the task at hand, so to speak. Without knowing the source of the voice, he began to wonder whether he should trust it or not. If the ship was indeed being boarded, Bill didn't want to face the threat head on, at least without a plan. The corridor up ahead ended at a T-intersection and he would have to either go left or right. He decided to go right and sneak up on the invaders from the other side.

"Take this left," said the voice.

"Damn it!" yelled Bill, stopping in his tracks. "Who the hell are you and how do I know I can trust you?"

"My apologies. I am the ship, *Tenuous Hope*."

"Huh? I didn't know the ship— um, you could talk." Bill tilted his head with a confused look on his face. Then he realized that the ship must have an AI that identified itself with the vessel as the physical manifestation of its consciousness. *Holy crap, this was beyond cool.*

"I usually don't engage with the help, but you are in the best position to purge the pending infestation."

"Me?" asked Bill in surprise. "What about Captain Rane? I'm sure I saw her return to the ship after seeing the rest of the crew away for planet leave."

"Captain Rane is currently indisposed. She is overseeing repairs to the quantum drive," answered the *Tenuous Hope* nonchalantly. "The repair crew has powered up a containment field as a safety precaution in case of explosion. No communications can penetrate the active field. We must deal with the intrusion unaided."

"I see," said Bill as the proverbial lead hit his belly. He was a maintenance guy, for crying out loud. Saving the ship wasn't on his list of duties, or at least he didn't think so. He most certainly wasn't prepared to save the day like some caped hero. "Um, *Tenuous Hope*?"

"Yes?"

"Your proper name is a bit awkward to say every time I need your attention. Can I just call you Ten?" asked Bill. "You can call me Bill. Deal?"

"Deal, Bill," agreed Ten.

"Well now that that's settled, what's next?"

"The infestation is spreading," replied Ten.

So, rodents or something, right? Bill could handle that. And if it was something worse, then bring it. He had resigned himself to the task at hand. If he failed this task and died, it would be no one's fault but his.

"Can you see where the intruders are at the moment?" asked Bill.

"Yes, I can see everything. We are losing precious time. I was directing you toward the armory first."

"Good idea," said Bill. "Lead the way."

"It is still left. Go left," directed Ten.

Bill took the left, then followed the gentle directions that came to him from his new personal life coach, emphasis on *life*. He ran in a staggered and random pattern from door to door, corridor to corridor.

"Why are you not taking a direct path?" asked Ten.

"I'm trying to evade detection by the enemy," explained Bill. "You know, evasive maneuvers."

"I do not know where you were trained, but your evasive antics are taking too long. The armory is now lost. You will encounter the intruders before reaching the weapons cache," said Ten.

Chagrined by his poor use of evasive tactics resulting in the loss of weapons, Bill stopped to take stock of his situation, but really to pout for being such a dork. This shit was so easy in role-playing video games.

"Any suggestions? I'm all ears," said Bill. At that moment, his left hand lit up like a Christmas tree. "All ears, and a hand, that is."

Instructed by Ten to approach the invading party from the side, he took a narrow service corridor off the main hallway, barely wide enough for two people to pass each other, and slowed as he neared the intruders.

He smelled them before he saw them. Wet dog. Muddy car. River fishing. All of those smells attacked his nose, and Bill halted. He peeked around the panel that separated him from the hatch and saw four enormous hairy hyena-looking creatures, standing on two legs, but panting like dogs in mid-July, drool dripping from their unnaturally long tongues. They held enormous weapons that looked deceivingly lightweight. Bill suspected the droolers weren't likely to take prisoners and he didn't want to risk it.

"They are the vermin!" exclaimed Ten, louder than necessary.

Four hyena men slowly turned as one to see Bill gawking at them.

"Crap. Thanks, Ten." Bill took a big gulp and turned away.

He ran around two corners, ducking into a cabin after sliding his hand over the entrance key. The door closed a millisecond before he heard the dogs run past.

"Whew," said Ten, and Bill could have sworn he heard a chuckle.

"I'm glad you're enjoying yourself," said Bill in between breaths. He closed his eyes and tried to will his heartbeat to slow. He sucked in air, taking deep breaths.

Out in the hallway, Bill could hear the intruders, and his ears sifted through their garbled dialogue to translate the conversation.

"The metal woman's mecphage research lab must be found," said one mutt. "You and you, fan out at the end of the hall. You, back track to the entry point and flank out to the other side of the ship. I will cover this path by cutting straight through. We meet in the rear junction."

Bill froze behind the cabin entranceway. Kimra. They were after Kimra's mecphage technology. What if they had already found her and hurt her in some way? He felt his innards surging, but it was more from fear this time than actual mecphage power rushing through him. Holding his breath, he slid his hand over the control pad to open the cabin door. No one was in the corridor, so he stepped out, closing the door behind him.

"Do you know who those guys are?" he asked Ten.

"Based on their morphology and behavioral patterns, the closest match in the database indicate they are of the planet Vladavir. Therefore, they must be Vlads," answered Ten.

"Hmm. Is there anything else in the database about them?" asked Bill.

"Checking the Toriff tourist database. One moment please," said Ten.

Bill let out an audible sigh as he waited impatiently for more information.

"To date, only males leave their planet. But all are hungry for meat. Any kind of meat. They stop here often and cause bloodshed and turmoil. A tourist travel advisory warning has been issued. You might want to—"

"How many of them are on Toriff?" interrupted Bill.

"That information is classified. In order to access that data from the Toriff Security and Protection Services, I would need level IV security clearance, which is a six month—"

"Can you hack into the system?" interrupted Bill again, this time with a bit more irritation in his voice.

"Yes, but it is a criminal offense and—"

"Do it. Just do it!" yelled Bill. Hearing his own voice, he realized it was a tad too loud and lowered the volume in order to avoid detection from the meat-hungry Vlads. With the exception of BG, Bill was 100% meat.

"One moment please," said Ten, ignoring Bill's little outburst. "According to official records, the total number of registered Vlads currently on Toriff, including those that have invaded the *Tenuous Hope*, is 17. However, the number of unregistered Vlads could be higher. It might be time now to—"

"What kind of weapon do I need to incapacitate them?" interrupted Bill yet again.

Ten made an audible sigh. "Their weapons are used only to stun their victims, not to kill. They like to kill with their teeth. But really, you need to—"

Bill froze, just as one of the Vlads rounded the corner and nearly ran him over. Before he could blink, Bill was locked in a neck wrench, his arm twisted painfully behind his back. Hot, horrible, almost tangible breath plumed around his face as hyena man panted and dripped stinky saliva onto his skinsuit.

"I so want to eat you right now," said the stinky cur.

"Well, now. Those are some fighting words," Bill gasped, his predicament reminding him of gym class where Coach Wiznewski used to show them classic wrestling holds and how to counteract them. Bill could never get out of those holds, no matter how much he practiced. Although his technique was sound, he never wanted to upset the balance of things for fear of retribution outside of gym class. Now, in this life and eat situation, he wished he had.

"Where is metal woman's research lab?" growled the Vlad, baring his huge incisors.

"Go to hell." Bill tried to make himself sound threatening, but his voice came out as a rubber mouse squeak.

The Vlad tightened his grip around Bill's neck, and Bill felt himself losing consciousness. In desperation, he grabbed the Vlad's arm that was doing the damage, pulled down on it, and at the same time torqued his body around the savage dingo, reversing the hold.

To Bill's surprise, unlike in high school, the counter maneuver came so easily. Almost like a little choreographed half-time band show. He gave himself a satisfied smile.

Grasping the Vlad by his hairy neck, Bill's prosthetic hand, or BG, was ablaze with lights, and the surges through his body, now a more familiar feeling, were alternately heating then cooling him. He closed his eyes as his opponent struggled. He felt the mecphages do their strength enhancing thing, or was it his confidence that got a boost?

Now all Bill had to do was outwit this character. And go the distance.

He strengthened his hold, but then his heart dropped at the sound of approaching footsteps, running toward them.

"Approaching footsteps," said Ten.

"Gee, thanks," Bill said. "Tell me something I don't know."

Bill grunted as the Vlad struggled to free himself from the stranglehold.

"The Vlads have destroyed the research lab to no avail. No crucial files have been accessed," announced Ten. "Your crewmates are returning as we speak."

All the while, Bill inched toward the cabin he had been hiding in before. He needed this smelly monster tucked away nice and tight. The Vlad twisted in his arms, growling and snapping. Bill clamped his real hand over the Vlad's mouth.

Bill closed his eyes again and focused on Kimra. The Vlads had targeted her lab and he needed to warn her. It was likely she was in the most danger now.

The moment Bill sensed Kimra's close proximity in his mind, he sent her a telepathic message.

Vlads on board! Hostile and wreaking havoc in your lab! Looking for mecphage research! Save yourself! Stay away and warn the others!

Bill felt a surge as the message hit the psychic airwaves. He concentrated and saw a vision of Kimra, Rikki, and at least ten crewmembers climbing the ramp to board the ship. They had pulled out weapons from their personal effects and were armed to the teeth.

Just as Kimra looked up in acknowledgement of his message, the remaining Vlads visiting Troit stormed toward the entrance, their orange scummy teeth bared and ready for battle.

Or dinner.

Chapter 18: Who Let the Dogs In?

Kimra stiffened and stood stock-still for just a moment, and although Bill couldn't see her with his physical eyes, his vision of her was blinding, all the same. Her metallic body gleamed like armor, and Bill watched her through closed eyes as she swung the rifle blaster around from its sling on her back in one deft movement.

Her eyes shone brightly, and Bill realized she was scanning information from everyone she had injected, including himself. She knew where he was, in the back of the ship, and she knew the strength of her enemies, now almost upon her.

The lead Vlad must have assumed she would be easily taken, because he approached her in an almost casual way, a bit out of breath from having run from the back of the ship. He reached for her with his claws, his weapon still slung across his back.

Kimra lowered her weapon, both arms at her side, seemingly defenseless. Then in one swift motion almost too fast to be seen by the naked eye, she side-stepped his grasp and brought her arm up at the same time.

The Vlad stopped in his tracks, confused as blood poured out of a deep gash in his face. He brought his clawed paw up to the wound, trying to quell the bleeding.

Kimra had sliced his face open. With a simple flick of her wrist, she slid a shining blade from a sheath on her thigh, and now it was stained with mangy mutt blood. Her team had mustered behind her, and then spread out to block the ship's entrance.

Still very much alive, the bone from his cheek exposed and blood spouting from his nostrils and through his teeth, the Vlad roared in surprise and rage, reaching back for his bulky gun. His eyes were crossed now, trying to focus together, but failing. They rolled around in his head while Kimra remained stoic, awaiting his next move.

Around him, Bill heard reactions, and for a second or two the combined voices sounded almost like a chorus. He heard Kimra, Rikki, Surrep, Cali, and the members of attending crew, all of them murmuring at first, then gradually separating in his thoughts so that he could discern what each was saying. But it didn't matter. They were saying pretty much the same thing.

"Preparedness is our first defense. We must always anticipate the unexpected. In emergency or battle, this is what will keep us alive." It was a beautiful symphony of voices, raised together like a melodic battle cry.

Bill nodded in understanding. This would explain why the crew brought their weapons with them on furlough.

Without giving the Vlad an opportunity to best her, Kimra plunged her blade into his heart. He fell just as his subordinates lumbered down the corridors, guns blazing.

Behind Kimra and her team, the Vlads that had not been among those who first boarded the ship came galloping up the ramp. They flung themselves, clumsy and tripping, through the outer door, grunting and drooling, and suddenly Bill Griffin knew he was actually needed.

"Not part of the solution, then part of the problem," he said, watching his prisoner and thinking of ways to contain him. How could he just leave this guy here? Or could he actually become a true beast and kill this warrior mutt?

That isn't who we are!

With BG still holding the furry dog-man, Bill scanned the small cabin for something to use as a binding. *It's your lucky day, hound. You get to live.* Then he noticed one of the buttons on his prosthetic started blinking a green light. It was marked with a 'W'. Bill had to do a double take as he could have sworn the button was not labelled earlier.

With his other hand, he managed to press the button on BG, and just as if he had conjured it up in his own mind, a set of sticky bungy cords spit out from his prosthetic fingers. They knitted themselves together while simultaneously wrapping around and around the struggling mongrel man's muzzle.

He moved BG down so that the Vlad's paws could be tightly bound together, too. Releasing some extra slack, Bill swung the free ends of the cords to a leg of one of the bunks, and just like that, the manic hyena man was tied by all fours to the bed. Spread eagle like in every bondage porn movie Bill had ever seen, well, the one movie. With a satisfied nod, Bill grabbed the Vlad's weapon, waved BG to open the door, and stepped stealthily into the corridor.

On silent orders, half of Kimra's team turned to face the dozen or so dog men. Cali led the defensive attack, her blue tentacles undulating with purpose. She reached out to the lead Vlad and wrapped one tentacle around his neck while another went straight for his crotch. His face bulged as he struggled for air and he twisted violently in her grip. As he slowly weakened, his eyes protruded, but Cali didn't stop.

Her little pursed beak-lips pinched together, and she tightened her grip on his neck until finally the Vlad's head completely popped off his body. Blood sprayed like a fountain over them both, staining Cali's blue skin red. She shook the Vlad's esophagus off like someone testing spaghetti on a wall.

Meanwhile, her other six tentacles busied themselves on more storming Vlads. With two of her appendages, she picked up one of the hyenas and smashed him against the entry corridor's walls. Another two tentacles grabbed an enemy by his feet and swung him in an arc to smash his skull. She reached with yet another to her face, now damp with perspiration, and dabbed it like a lady at the opera. It certainly was a busy dog-day afternoon.

Rikki wrapped her body all the way around one of the hulking enemies and squeezed. Her tongue tested the air and her nostrils flared at his canine odor until finally she closed them into slits. Bill watched her through his newly found vision, even while he ran from the rear of the ship. It was like watching a movie while in rocket-flight, with so much going on around him but also in his new vision's screen. Like playing two video games at once.

Rikki's victim succumbed to her tight embrace. The bones in his back snapped, followed by each arm and leg, and it sounded to Bill like that annoying jock in high school, the one who would crack his knuckles in study session. Briefly, Bill's thoughts flashed back to that hometown scene he had wandered through in three beautiful dimensions, back in the K-torium. It seemed like days ago instead of one dogshit-filled afternoon.

Rikki stuffed a smooth fist into the Vlad's mouth to stifle his final screams just as Captain Rane arrived. The snake woman gave a whimsical smile to Rane, then moved to disable another fetid attacker.

Captain Rane didn't have the patience to take on just one of these creatures at a time. She opened fire with her weapon, careful to aim only above and behind the immediate skirmish toward the pack still coming from beyond the perimeter. She mowed a few down, yet more advanced. Anyone attacking her ship deserved no quarter.

Taking her time with her aim once again, the beautiful green-skinned captain exhaled as she pulled the trigger. Like the last time, it was as simple as target practice. Most of her six self-assigned marks went down as they succumbed to the lethal blasts, blood covering the ground and surrounding areas. Throughout the firefight, she kept her lips pressed together in a tight line, her facial expression pure business-like.

Surrep bent over one of Sanya Rane's victims as he sobbed for his mother. She ran a careful finger over some of his teeth. Then she turned, touching her eight breasts, and faced two oncoming Vlads from inside the ship. Bill knew just then that he would be late to this party. These were two of the original intruders. He watched in horror as he ran toward battle.

Surrep grabbed her top two breasts and squeezed. It reminded Bill of a field trip in elementary school on Earth, when they visited an ancient farm and watched a man milk a real cow. As Surrep pulled her nipples out, a green liquid sprayed onto the faces of the lumbering Vlads. They screeched in pain and clawed at their faces.

"Acid?" asked Bill as he approached.

"Something like that, yes," answered Surrep. "Actually, more like intense pepper spray or nerve intensifier."

Bill watched Surrep clean her bosom until another struggle caught his attention. The final three Vlads held Kimra against the wall of a threshold, and one had an arm pressing firmly on her diaphragm. Another Vlad had his fingers in Kimra's mouth, stretching her lips the way little kids do when they want to make a face. Her teeth bared in anger or pain, or both. Her breasts heaved from the pressure on her torso.

Without thinking, Bill leapt onto the back of the closest Vlad, and desperately looked at his adversary's weapon.

"Ten, how do I work this?" he yelled.

"Under the barrel. Squeeze."

He did as Ten instructed, and the weapon fired a laser blast, but Bill didn't think he actually hit anything. He rode his Vlad like a bucking horse though, and that wrenched the enemy's fingers out of Kimra's mouth. She gave a painful looking grimace at Bill as he got thrown like an empty pop bottle into the air. As he sailed, Bill saw Kimra compose herself with steely determination. Her eyes went dark and he knew she was once more focused on the skirmish.

Bill still wanted to help, but just as he reached for his now familiar 'W' button, he heard a grunt as the Vlad he had been riding took a heavy fall into the other Vlad who still held Kimra by the midriff.

Rikki had come up behind the fallen Vlad and Bill watched in fascinated horror as the beautiful snake woman unhinged her jaw. It fell open like her face had suddenly broken, but she gave him a reassuring glance as she indelicately took the Vlad's head into her mouth.

Scrambling away from that crazy scene and wrenching himself from the ground, Bill lunged at the Vlad who was still pressed up against Kimra. With BG blazing colors and sparks, he grasped the Vlad by the neck and was astounded to see the beast hanging from Bill's arm without much effort on his part.

But the Vlad had a trick up his sleeve or dress or whatever the hell he was wearing, and Bill gasped as the squirming Vlad swung a dagger toward Bill's exposed neck. Kimra, recovering from her loss of breath, blocked the dagger's path and punched the Vlad in the snout with incredible force. Cartilage and snot gore flowed down Bill's arm, making him gag at the disgusting bloody goo.

"Don't look," instructed Kimra as Bill dropped the hyena carcass to the ground.

"Don't look? Don't look? Which one do we not want to look at here, Kimra?" he asked, a crazy expression in his eyes as he smeared the blood from BG onto the once pristine floor.

"It would behoove you to avert your gaze from Rikki in this particular moment, Bill Griffin," Kimra said after a little cough.

Which, of course, meant Bill had to look directly at Rikki.

"I'm so glad that I'm on your side," Bill said, wincing as he saw the last of the Vlad's kicking hairy feet disappear into Rikki's contorted mouth.

Rikki saw him watching and gave him a little apologetic shrug. Her body had taken on the stretched-out form of the Vlad himself, who was still, grotesquely and alarmingly, struggling inside her. She fell, exhausted, to the floor and closed her eyes. She looked like Bill's great grandfather, back when they had celebrated Thanksgiving with a feast of turkey and every imaginable wonderful side dish. Drowsy and full, Rikki covered her mouth to let out a soft burp.

"Thank you, Bill Griffin," said Kimra in a soft, almost feminine voice. "You were most helpful in containing the intruders. For the love of Lorde Velt, I hope you remain alive and on our side."

Bill wondered briefly why Kimra's god sounded familiar, but he was exhausted, grossed out after watching Rikki devour the Vlad live and whole, and just too emotionally fragmented. He forced a pensive smile at Kimra and turned away, trying not to slip on the bloodied floor.

Chapter 19: And Then There Was One

Bill swallowed the bile that insisted on seeping into the back of his mouth, wiped his lips onto his suit, and checked the fallen Vlads to make sure they were all really, truly dead. With a bloodied BG finger to his lips, he motioned to Kimra that there was still one hungry hyena just down the hall, locked in the cabin. Kimra touched both hands to her hair as if to un-muss it, then followed him.

Last he saw, Cali was slapping dead Vlads with her suction-cupped hands, Captain Rane was closing up the entry way, scanning the surface of Troit for more incoming enemies, and Rikki was still digesting on the floor. Others gingerly stepped around her.

Again, with his finger to his lips, Bill stood before the door where he'd left the only remaining Vlad soundly trussed. They had to be careful in case dog breath had managed to loosen his bonds. Kimra gave an efficient nod and pulled a shining knife from her thigh.

"Something you might find interesting," announced Ten, just before Kimra and Bill opened the door to the cabin. "Vlad testicles? They can be found behind the ears, believe it or not."

"No way," said Bill.

"Way," Ten said.

Bill looked at Kimra and realized that she could hear this conversation, too. She pretended to be readying herself but her metallic face gave a hint of some gears turning in her head.

"This guy? The one behind the door? Only has one," Ten continued.

Kimra and Bill exchanged a knowing look that somewhat sealed the fate of the unsuspecting Vlad. Bill almost felt sorry for him as only another guy could.

"The testicle is behind the left ear. It is very, very small. The size of a peanut. Without its shell. You can bring this one down easily by just grabbing that ear or slashing it."

Bill could have sworn he heard Ten clear her throat.

"It is my belief that the threat of torture can be worse than the torture itself. Am I right?" inquired Bill.

Both Ten and Kimra remained silent, but he could tell it was a silence of endorsement. The worst of the attack was long past, and adrenaline rushes were starting to fade. When Bill raised his arm to touch the door control panel, he noticed several buttons on BG that hadn't been lit up before. Orange and indigo and maroon, they looked like someone had hot glued jellybeans onto his arm. Some were flashing, others threw off a steady light. Bill noted the additional hues and touched the control pad to open the door at its slowest speed.

A lime-green button flashed the brightest with the letter 'P' appearing on it.

Bill looked at Kimra, shaking his head, just as he reached around his wrist, and pressed the lime-green button.

Out from his thumb and his index fingers, metal pincers sprouted. When he made the *okay* sign to Kimra, his fingers looked like those spaghetti tongs his aunt Em used on Sunday nights. He felt a pang of longing in his gut, thinking of family dinners, but Kimra cleared her throat and Bill caught a delightful whiff of WD-40 to break his de-railed train of thought.

As the door opened, the Vlad threw himself at it, very much awake and alive, and Bill felt a renewal of energy as his mind went once again to the very real possibility of his own death. Somehow, the Vlad had partially broken through his restraints. Without knowing his conscious reason, Bill opened his mouth and let forth a crazy war cry, the kind he used back when he was a kid fighting imaginary Orcs in his front yard. Kimra raised two steely eyebrows, and together they stormed the cabin.

Kimra was a whirlwind. She ran behind the Vlad as he was diving toward Bill and locked him in a metallic hold, his unnaturally long arms tangled together behind his back. She calmly reached into a silver satchel on her ass and pulled out metal restraints. It was over before Bill knew what was happening.

"We need him in the research lab," Kimra said matter-of-factly.

"Yes. Research lab. Don't know where that is."

"Follow me," Kimra said. "It is the room where we first made acquaintance."

"Ah, of course. Research," said Bill. He looked down at his pincers and clacked them open and closed a couple of times.

"Tenderly," said Ten.

"Tenderly?" Bill echoed aloud. "No fucking way am I going tenderly on this one." He grimaced at Kimra and she shrugged.

"Just do it," she said.

Bill reached behind the Vlad's left ear, found a little soft nugget pouch of flesh, and gently squeezed. The Vlad fell to his knees, unable to utter a groan much less a respectable howl.

"Let up a bit, Bill Griffin," Kimra said. "We want him awake and very much engaged when he gets there. Do what Ten says. Go gentle, if you please." She cleared her throat and Bill inhaled.

"Oh, I thought I had," he said.

Kimra gave Bill a doubting look, complete with eyeroll before they strong-armed the Vlad through the ship's passageways and back to the laboratory where Bill had first met Kimra. Again, it seemed like eons ago. Maybe time moved slowly in space or Bill needed more oxygen, because this shit was surreal. While they walked, Bill questioned his sanity, yet his tong fingers kept a gentle but firm grip on the Vlad's little ear testicle. Kimra asked questions.

"Did any of them give clues as to what their goals were, Bill Griffin? Were any details mentioned regarding my research?"

"Um, sorry, Kimra. I was kind of distracted by their teeth and their breath, and how fucking big they are. I don't think I was a very good listener this afternoon," Bill said. He gave the ear nugget a little pinch of anger and the Vlad managed a whimper. Instinctively, Bill's real hand covered his own crotch.

"Did they inject you or Qeet or Nialme? Were any fluids shared?" Kimra's stare bored into Bill's eyes.

"Unfortunately, no. I mean, about the body fluids. No fluids on board between anyone."

"Bill Griffin. I'm talking specifically about injected fluids. Needles, not body parts. I am looking for chemical break-ins, any compromised research." She sighed a little and shook her head.

"Oh. Gosh, no. No needles from the Vlads. And again, I'm sorry I didn't hear anything. I was just starting to get used to Ten's disembodied voice, and it was a little off-putting."

One of Kimra's eyebrows raised in question. "Ten?"

"You know," answered Bill. "Tenuous Hope? The AI? I call her Ten."

A look of comprehension washed over Kimra's metallic face. "Ah, an interesting quirk that humans like to shorten things. Efficient. I like it."

The Vlad struggled and grunted, causing Bill to slightly increase the pressure on the ear gonad.

"How did you manage to subdue this one when you first ran into him? With the tongs?" she asked.

He snorted in memory. "No. It was actually quite remarkable. I was stronger than I ever imagined, and filaments came out of my fingers to tie him up. I also got to use some wrestling moves from high school. Even though I never made the team. I remembered some moves instinctively. You know." When the Vlad snickered, Bill pinched the nugget a little less tenderly and was rewarded with Vlad puke, smelly and meaty.

Kimra stopped short, having arrived at the research lab.

It was all but destroyed. The exam table was overturned, medical equipment and cords were ripped from walls, tubes and beakers, and sterile pads littered the floor. Kimra walked on silent soles to the far corner of the room.

As Bill watched with wide eyes and open mouth, she reached into her metallic skirt with one hand, and with her eyes closed and head thrown back, she moved that hand like a magician reaching into his hat for a white rabbit. When she withdrew her hand, she gave her fingers a long luxurious sniff, then lovingly, tenderly even, touched the wall.

As if in answer to a secret code, the wall started to move, not sideways like a normal portal, but inwards, like an old-fashioned mystery's bookcase. Bill didn't even notice. His eyes were still glued onto Kimra's hand.

What on Earth just happened?

He must have broadcasted his thoughts telepathically because Kimra looked over her shoulder at him in response. Her lips didn't move, but he got her message loud and clear.

Oh, Bill. No one is on Earth anymore.

The Vlad interrupted Bill's revelry, jerking his head away from the violating pincers. He spit a bit of leftover vomit onto BG before Bill snapped out of the damn-the Earth-is-gone-but-Kimra-had-her-hand-down-her-pants fog fantasy. He readjusted his grip on the creature's ear testicle.

Kimra was still scanning the research lab, assessing the extensive damage. Bill saw her eyes flashing, as she took photographs of the destroyed equipment. Shattered glassware covered the floor, the controls of the spectrometer were smashed beyond repair, and the DNA sequencer sputtered sporadically while analyzing irregularly shaped brown globs that could only be fecal matter.

Bill listened to her disjointed kind of telepathic inventory as he tried to gauge her sense of rage but could only detect a detached feeling of calmness.

"Your… uh, dare I call them your 'people', sir?" She narrowed her silver eyes at the Vlad. "They have ransacked my industry here."

Bill blinked. Following Kimra's speech patterns was like a constant little challenge. But he liked it.

She continued. "I will assume others are waiting in transit to follow you. I will further assume that, while you and your current roustabouts are neutralized, those who deign to join us might still have curiosities to assuage." She gave the Vlad a thin-lipped smile.

The Vlad suddenly stopped fidgeting beside Bill. Bill's eyes followed the hyena-man's eyes into the new room that Kimra had so unconventionally opened. Gurneys and racks and steely-probed equipment lined the walls of what was most certainly a modern-day interrogation room of sorts, a persuasion chamber in space.

Bill had read about these in conspiracy newsletters and espionage fiction books, but he never thought they existed. His stomach lurched as he surveyed the promise of pain and horror on levels he could never imagine emanating from oh so many inanimate, yet inventive, objects.

The Vlad stood up taller, closed his mouth, cleared his throat, and started yammering. Apparently, he was very familiar with the purpose of such rooms.

"I could be useful to you. Alive. You will be no wiser with me dead." He looked beseechingly at Bill, then back at Kimra. "I was just doing my job, for Balzar's sake! Think of how you could use me! I could go back, be a spy for you!"

Bill just looked at Kimra, not believing their luck. With the way hyena man withstood the pain of having his testicle crushed, Bill thought they had a tough job ahead of them.

Do not look too surprised. The reputations of these persuasion chambers precede themselves. It is usually just enough to show that you have such a room to persuade a captive to divulge all information. In fact, most of these artifacts are just for show. But they can be easily converted to active duty should the situation demand.

Bill slowly nodded his head in comprehension to Kimra's telepathic message. He understood precisely what she was saying. Ouch.

The Vlad's eyes desperately darted from a noose contraption that was strung up to a swinging gate, then back to what was definitely an advanced version of a pillory, its holes for head and appendages gaping wide. Bill shuddered even though he knew it wouldn't be needed, wouldn't be used.

"Be a spy for us? Do not make me regurgitate my mid-circadian meal, sir," Kimra said, shaking her head. Apparently, the thought that the mercenary would break an unwritten code of sorts, was not convincing enough.

She jutted her chin toward Bill as she traded places with him, placing her hand over his extended prosthetic and grasping the Vlad by his ball. Briefly, Bill felt the surge of energy that came from her touch, the touch that had just recently returned from her crotch dive. He inhaled her WD-40 scent, sighed, and nodded.

"You must leave us now, Bill Griffin," Kimra said as the Vlad whimpered under her squeeze. "Thank you for your assistance in an otherwise unpleasant day. Allow me to ascertain the truth as only I can. Perhaps you could find Nialme and Qeet? See to their wellbeing?"

He nodded dumbly at her, the pincers in BG receding back into its fingers, and as the secret door

started to close in front of him, he thought he saw her
lick her fingers.

Chapter 20: Hope is a Battlefield

Bill put BG over his nose and mouth as he made his way through the hallways from the research lab. As he approached the *Tenuous Hope's* entryway, he could see more crew members were now on board and busying themselves mopping up the blood and entrails left behind from the failed invasion.

The Floomba, a crablike android, low to the ground and sporting googly eyes that rolled as if in ecstasy, swept through the halls and galleys, sucking up the remnants of tissue and blood after the crew took care of the first big-chunk clean up.

Buckets and mops and assorted cleaning supplies lay at regular intervals, and the mood of the crew was positively upbeat, reminiscent of a post-prom clean-up. Feathered women laughed with their scaled shipmates as they scooped up intestines and slopped them into trash receptacles, and Bill smiled at them as he tiptoed through their slick workspaces.

At the entryway, Rikki still lay in a food coma. Someone must have nudged her up against the wall so that others could get past her. Bill reflected on his first visit to Surreptitious, when Rikki had turned down his invitation to join him for a meal. She had said she would catch something on the run. The thought of that prophetic comment made him chuckle.

Bill heard Rikki moan softly, so he leaned down to check on her. When he touched her yellow scaled forehead, her hand whipped forward from where it had been resting on her belly. She grabbed BG, which immediately lit up.

"Tssst," she said, her eyes glazed and only halfway open. "Sssmooth it for me? Nice and sssoft?" She took his hand and rubbed it over the bump that was once a nearly seven-foot hyena warrior. Bill remembered his Gram's old bloodhound, how the dog had always flopped down on her back and spread her legs for a belly rub. It was kind of embarrassing, then and now, but he acquiesced and ran his fingers up and down the length of Rikki's stretched-out torso.

"Wow, Rikki," he said after clearing his throat. "You're a fast digester! This guy is down to the size of a July watermelon! Pretty impressive." He smiled as she blinked in appreciative silence. Then their eyes locked, and Bill's mouth dried up. BG reflected his body's confusion; the jelly-bean lights were flashing in crazy patterns and one button, a new one, Bill thought in a brief moment of mental clarity, even made a little beeping sound.

His eyes had left Rikki's for a moment but returned to find hers steady and wide. Her tongue came out in a languid point and she blinked, long and slow. A tremor of excitement rippled through him, but at the same time, the adrenaline of genuine fear whooshed down to his pelvis. He had, after all, seen what Rikki was capable of putting into her mouth. All at once.

"Um. I hope you're back to your old self soon, Rikki. That was quite a mouthful. The Vlad, I mean."

He cleared his throat again and looked around, anywhere but into her eyes. "I sure hope you're up and around on your ship legs real, real soon. But for now? Kimra's orders, I've got to check in on Qeet and Nialme. I'll, um, probably be back this way later, when you're back to… uh, normal."

"I will sssee you later, Bill Griffin," Rikki said, her lips curling up and around her still outstretched tongue. "You and your wondrousss hand."

He rose and scurried away, actually scurried, he thought, like a small animal who had escaped the jaws of a dreaded predator. Man, what he wouldn't have given for ten minutes alone in bed with Rikki. Or even out of bed. But then again, he hoped he would never be alone with Rikki. Back and forth his mind went until he finally reached the front of the closet door where he had left Qeet and Nialme.

Rapping on the side of the cupboard, he shouted that everything was safe, and when he pulled out the towels that had covered them, the enormous tetherball that was Nialme rolled out and bounced onto the floor. As it rolled, Bill heard the chirping that was unmistakably Qeet. On top of the ball, the voice was loud and squawking, and then as Nialme rolled over and Qeet was squashed on the bottom, the yelp was muffled. Bill smiled as he listened.

"mr. bill griffIn, hELP MR. BILL GRIFFIN, QEEt in here, mR BILL!"

"All right, hey, Nialme, stop!" Bill reached down to touch her solid outer layer. She unrolled and looked up at him with just a hint of mischief in her eyes.

Qeet popped out and somehow quickly accessed the ship's recording of the battle from an information panel close by. He watched the play by play of the battle of the Vlads, listening to the crew's conversations in six times normal speed. Then he filled Nialme in as best as he could, given his limited vocabulary, and now was chittering nonstop about the enemy's decimation.

"Gotta see. Gotta see, Bill Griffin! Eater Vlads dead dead dead. Qeet no pikelet!" He fluttered his wings and squawked before transporting to just outside the cabin's threshold, then bouncing straight up into the air in excitement. "Blood and guts of bad eaters. Uglier than Troiters. Gotta GO SEE!" He fluttered his wings and half-squawked, then he was gone.

When Bill looked back at Nialme, he saw her eyes scanning him, and he stopped to get his bearings on his body. It was covered in blood and goo, and he could smell himself, a strange mix of sweat and copper and rotting meat. Nialme carefully reached out to touch his hand. She lifted her lip in not so well-disguised disgust.

"I think, Bill Griffin, we must once again visit the water falling cave, the shower you introduced me to earlier." She wrinkled her nose and he nodded as he laughed.

"Thank you," she said as they walked. "For making a safe spot for Qeet and me." She forgot her hesitations about the goo and gave him a warm furry hug. Slug-sized bits of flesh dropped from her breasts when they finally pulled apart, and she retracted in revulsion.

He reached into the shower stall and started the steaming hot water. She glanced from BG then to his eyes.

"Those clothes? Put them outside your cabin tonight. Fweena will get them and replace them with a fresh set."

"Fweena?" Bill asked with a snort.

"Fweena, the maintenance factotum. You would love her. Everyone loves her. It's how she gets paid, actually. Everyone spends time on top of Fweena. She drinks sweat."

"Wha—," Bill started to ask, but she was already getting wet in the shower and he didn't want to waste a moment. He stripped off his entrail-soaked clothes and joined her.

They took their time lathering each other with Hope Soap, a luxurious bubbly mixture that came out of the shower's porous walls. Nialme was meticulous in her ministrations and Bill luxuriated in how she was able to wash away the dread of the day as well as the blood and guts. When they finished in the shower, he realized there were no more towels hanging on the outer rails.

"You do not need towels when you have me, Bill," Nialme purred. She started on his toes and delicately licked every inch of his body with her rough tongue until not a drop of water remained. He looked down at BG and smiled sheepishly at her when he realized that his prosthetic hand wasn't the only part of him that had gone off. When he started to apologize, Nialme licked her lips and shushed him.

"But how about you? Your, uh, fur is still wet, and I can't do that kind of crazy action with my tongue."

Nialme batted her eyes at him and he stammered, "Not that I wouldn't want to, but you know what I mean. My tongue doesn't work like yours."

She stood then and sighed. Something about her sigh must have set off an automated surround dry, because the next thing Bill knew, hot winds blew around them, kicking up Nialme's fur. Her coat frizzed out so much under the internal whirlwind that she looked like a cartoon porcupine who had been struck by lightning.

Bill covered his mouth to hide his snicker, but when Nialme looked in the mirror, she was clearly horrified. She crouched to the floor and tried to roll herself into a ball, but her tail wouldn't stretch completely over the mop of frizzed hair, and just the sight of her being ungainly and awkward caught Bill's sense of humor. He wholeheartedly gave in to it. Grabbing his bare belly, he let out a loud laugh. Without holding anything back, he let tears stream down his cheeks.

How long had it been since he'd had a true belly laugh? Nialme's indignation made him laugh even harder, and she marched back into the shower to start all over.

A crackle came over the ship-wide comm system, interrupting Bill's amusement.

"Bill Griffin, please report to the bridge. Bill Griffin? Bridge, please," said a disembodied voice through hidden speakers.

"Blech," Bill said. "Sounds like a little green monster captain is requesting my presence. And I'll have to put these gross clothes back on."

Nialme couldn't hear him in the running shower, but he could have sworn he saw her stick out her little sandpaper tongue at him.

Fair enough.

Chapter 21: Hold My Hand

Bill entered the bridge to find the important players already there, aggregated on the upper platform, right by the entrance. He squeezed in behind Rikki, who was upright and sporting only a baby-bump-sized bulge. The Vlad was nearly digested. Bill shot her a timid smile, part of him still a bit jittery about becoming her next meal, whether it be next week or next month. He could have sworn the look she sent back to him was mixed with a fuzzy telepathic message that reminded him of someone longing for a pork chop.

He closed his eyes and concentrated on what Captain Rane was saying. She stood center deck, hands on hips, green skin glowing and red hair neatly curled, as if she had just stepped out of the shower. The thought of the shower threatened to break his focus yet again, with memories of Nialme's tongue dancing all over his body, but he shut his eyes for the moment and just listened.

"Our mission, as most of you already know, was side-tracked by our ill-advised attempt to rescue the blue rock before Balzar got to it." Sanya Rane sent a sneer in Bill's direction and he turned his head both ways to look behind him.

Rane sighed and continued. "Now it is time to return to what is truly important. We must reach Marzz as soon as is Earthly possible, pun intended. Ryval has communicated that all accessible intel has been gathered and is ready for dissemination. Meanwhile, the concern is that Balzar and his cronies have placed trackers on Lorde Velt's previous and current contacts, which of course leads back to Marzz himself." She flipped her red curls over her shoulder and crossed her arms. "And us."

She let the silence settle. Bill got the definite feeling that Captain Sanya Rane loved her a big dose of drama. He cleared his throat and raised BG.

"What?" Rane asked impatiently.

"Um, sorry. Newcomer here," Bill said. "Is Marzz a planet? A system? And who is Ryval, please? And maybe Lord Velt, while we're at it? That name keeps bouncing around and I could swear I've heard of it somewhere before. Or read it, maybe, sometime before, if you follow me."

"Good God." Rane exhaled through her contorted mouth to send a curly red tendril up and off her face. "You do know your way to K-torium, correct, Earthling Griffin? Perhaps you could bury yourself there and do some research on the *Tenuous Hope* and our missions, past and present? Then perhaps we won't spend undue futures rehashing data to keep you informed?"

"I'll take this, Captain," Kimra interjected. She stood, shiny and silver in the corner of the bridge with an electronic device perched on one hip. "Meanwhile, in a few words, Bill, Ryval Marzz is the name of a key cluster member who has been assigned to gather intel in Rhapsodic Bohem, a system not far from here. Our mission is to collect him and the data he has found before Balzar does."

Kimra examined a display on her device and tapped a metallic finger on it, deep in thought. "As many of you might not know, but of course Bill Griffin *does* know, one Vlad was spared the recent battle." Here she gave Captain Rane a very pointed stare. "Fortunately, Mr. Griffin detained one intact Vlad so that I could extract intel from him in the research lab. We appreciate your foresight, Bill, and what I learned in the last hour has certainly been enlightening."

Bill felt a warm flush wash through to his cheeks and he knew the grin he sent to Kimra was goofy, not just the grateful smile he had intended.

"It seems the Vlads who attacked the *Hope* today had been so instructed by Blue Balzar himself," Kimra continued. "I was able to confirm that Balzar is indeed tracking Lorde Velt's known associates, and the Vlads were on a mission to break into the research lab. They were tasked with stealing the mecphage research and development of the *lr-DNA* project, which clusters our collective minds and enables us to communicate with each other telepathically within certain parameters."

Sanya Rane cocked her head and raised an eyebrow, casting a glance at Bill then back to Kimra.

"I'm thinking," she said, "That we go full throttle to get to Marzz as quickly as the *Hope* will allow, tuck him safely away, then find a decent faraway asteroid to hide behind until the threat dies down. Please return to your cabins and rest. Rhapsodic Bohem is just around the corner. Seven, eight hours tops. Buckle up because we will be boosting. And Kimra? I would speak with you privately, please."

Bill waited in the corridor for Kimra, peeking into the bridge once in a while to see what was going on between the two women. Both were shaking their heads, both had furrowed brows, but he couldn't hear their words. Bill tried to listen telepathically, but it seemed like he was being purposely shut out.

When Kimra finally emerged from the bridge and they started back to their cabins, Bill leaned in and asked, "So? Did your knuckles get slapped?"

"I beg your pardon?" Kimra stopped walking and held up her metallic hands, flexing the fingers on each.

"Just an Earth saying, I suppose," Bill said in a voice that gave away his sadness. "Did you get in trouble with the Captain about me? Or about saying too much back there?"

"Oh, no, all is well, Bill."

"So, this Lord Velt? Who is he, really?"

"He? Oh," Kimra turned to him, and Bill suddenly noticed a glob of gray the size of a golf ball, slimy and almost slug-like, resting just above her cleavage. He interrupted her answer by pointing to it. BG lit up instantly.

"Um, Kimra? What's *that*?"

Kimra looked down onto her uniform and her skin circuitry lit up in answer. "Ooh, jelly on the side, please!" She scooped the gray gunk onto her index finger and popped it into her mouth with an uncharacteristic grin.

"What was that?" Bill said, after an involuntary gack sound came up from his throat.

"That, Bill Griffin, was Vlad brain."

"No. Way. Brains?"

"Mmm. Like having a double espresso for me. Like eating two plates of your pikelets, extra syrup, at midnight. We waste nothing here, Bill. Come, let us get settled."

He followed slightly behind her. "Like a totally green ship, right? Like everything is recycled?" She made an *um-hm* sound and he thought not for the first time about the acid that Surrep had shot out of her breasts during the battle, immediately after she had extracted maple syrup for him at breakfast. He shuddered. He seemed to be doing that a lot lately.

"Captain Rane told me we will be stopping at the planet Little Pekkur on our way to Rhapsodic Bohem. There is someone who claims to have information that even our beloved Ryval Marzz hasn't been able to access, and we need all the assistance we can get."

"Wait, there's a planet named 'Little Pekkur'?" asked Bill.

"That is correct."

"Why?"

"Why not?"

"No, Kimra. I mean, where did it get its name?"

"I have no historical colonization data on Little Pekkur but most of the inhabitants migrated from Big

Pekkur according to the combined governmental Big and Little Pekkur heads of state," said Kimra.

"Now you're telling me there is a Big Pekkur and Big and Little Pekkur heads of state? You're killing me, Kimra. I couldn't make this shit up if I tried." laughed Bill.

"Both planets are odd places, but I do not understand your amusement. The inhabitants stand less than three-feet high, so the Pekkur populations on both planets are diminutive. In any case, we need you rested and prepared to face another challenge, Bill Griffin. You proved in today's battle that you are a valuable resource. Even the captain has to give your contribution a nod. I shall leave you to rest well."

They had arrived in front of his cabin, and he could hear Qeet chirping away behind the closed door.

"Wait. I have another question," said Bill.

Kimra made an audible sigh but caught herself and waited.

"It's about my hand. BG," Bill said, holding his prosthetic in front of her face.

"Is that what you call it?" she asked with some amusement in her demeanor. She shook her head slightly and said, "Never mind. What about it?"

"It knows things." Bill hesitated, trying to find the words without sounding ungrateful. "Like it's reading my mind. Buttons appear, labelled with letters."

"That is normal," said Kimra. "The mecphage tech enables your brain to communicate directly with your prosthetic, or BG as you have abbreviated it. It should feel like a natural extension of your body."

Bill raised his right hand and wiggled his real fingers. "But I had to use this hand, my good hand, to push the buttons and make shit happen with BG."

"Oh, Bill Griffin, believe me, that little appendage right there?" She pointed to his right hand and smirked. "That is *not* your 'good hand'. Your good hand is BG." She looked at the prosthetic with a mechanic's pride in her eyes. "Let us take a closer look in my lab, shall we?" And she led the way down the hall.

When they got to the lab, Bill noticed that it was clean, pristine even. The exposed circuitry was once again in place and functioning. Bill saw no blood, and, thankfully, no brains. Kimra waved at the exam table, and Bill jumped onto it, holding BG out for her to look at.

"Let us see," she said, examining the buttons, none of which were lit up. "Tell me about your concerns with pushing the buttons with your other hand."

"Well, I guess it's hard to explain," said Bill. "Mostly it seems like it lights up in an intense moment, or a last-ditch kind of emergency. And then I have to free up my other hand to press a button. It's awkward."

"I suppose that's my fault for basing part of the design on an old Earth animated visual representation I found. My limited time did not allow me to do the proper amount of research required."

Kimra looked at Bill and he fell silent. Then suddenly it seemed like the answer came to her, like an actual lightbulb went off in her head. Her lips twitched.

"Bill Griffin, this will not hurt a bit."

He watched her grab BG and rip it off his arm right before he passed out. Again.

Chapter 22: Night Shift

When he finally opened his eyes, Bill felt for one impossible moment like he was waking up in the spaceship for the very first time. Had it been days or weeks? It was like none of the recent past had even happened, like it had been a sitcom's final episode, where everyone realized this whole thing had been nothing but a long, weird dream. Or nightmare.

But no, he knew the name of the pesky creature sitting on his forehead, chirping and flapping his little triangular wing arms. Some of Qeet's feather furs were shedding and landing on Bill's face, fluttering up his nostrils, making him sneeze.

"Bounce you, Bill Griffin."

"It's 'bless you', Qeet, not 'bounce you,' and anyway, I'm questioning the existence of God right now and don't want to be blessed. Or bounced, for that matter. Get off!" He waved his hands over his face and caught sight of BG. A new BG. A new and beautiful, sleek BG.

He sat up straight, finally waving Qeet away, and took a moment to examine his new combo arm and hand prosthetic. It was BG, all right, but definitely an upgraded model.

"I'm thinking you, my friend, are quite the tool. Helping me do things right, right?" Was it possible to have a crush on one of your own appendages? Well, duh.

He flexed the fingers, now more slender and streamlined than the former model. He rotated the wrist and the arm. The buttons were gone. As he wondered what had been added to replace the buttons, a transparent display or screen lit up before his eyes. Wherever he looked, the display remained in the same position within his field of vision.

I must be the only one who can see it.

A few moments later, the display disappeared while Bill continued to admire BG 2.0. It was definitely smaller than the previous one. And it had hairs and pores.

What function would the hairs and pores provide? Bill wondered.

Then it hit him like a ton of moon rocks. BG 2.0 looked almost like a mirror-image of his right arm and hand. It was what his real left arm and hand would have looked like if it had not been so tragically torn from his body.

"Larm Clock, Bill Griffin! Time to shine and rise!" Qeet fluttered back down to perch in Bill's lap. He looked up with his huge googly eyes and gave a beaky little smile. "Mission Possible start soon!"

"Wait, what?" Bill had not finished admiring his new prosthetic and thinking of how normal his life would had been if he had gotten it sooner.

"*Tennyson Hope* nears destiny nation, Bill Griffin. It's Rhapsody in Blue Time!"

Bill shook his head and rubbed his eyes. "Crazy bird monkey," he mumbled. "I think you're going for Rhapsodic Bohem, right? But we're stopping on Little Pekkur first."

"Been that done there, Mr. Bill. While Bill Griffin sleeps, *Hope* stops at Little Pekkur. Good food on Little Pekkur. Sweet Treats. Too bad you missed. Nearly there, Bill Griffin. Must dress. Fresh clothes, no blood, no guts, no vom." Qeet teleported over to Bill's shoulder, then vanished and reappeared on Bill's right foot. In a flash, Bill watched as BG shot out and grabbed Qeet, who instantly stopped chattering. They both became still, looking into each other's eyes.

"The tool has spoken," Bill said. "I didn't even know I could move that fast! What did she do to me, anyway? And how long have I been out?"

"Kimra and Captain wait, Mr. Bill. They can say what happened to Tool Hand Luke. Now, Missionary Positions! Must bounce to lab. We bounce now!"

Bill dressed and let Qeet ride on his shoulder as he made his way to the research lab.

"You're getting quite the urban Earthling vocab, there, my little friend," Bill said.

"Qeet watch many exstink Earthling tube vision," Qeet said, puffing his chest out a bit in pride. "Sometimes, vids are in gray. No rainbow!"

"Ah, yes," Bill said, patting Qeet on his little back. He wasn't really paying much attention though, noticing instead how little he actually had to concentrate to find his way around the ship now.

"Watch, Mr. Bill, Qeet roll up sexy and smart like Nialme," Qeet said. "Qeet bounce straight up like rocket, but Nialme, she spin like ball." He rolled his little fuzzy body, now white like the corridors, into a tufted muff, and tried to bounce like Nialme.

Bill watched the little creature struggle to ball himself up. "Some things, Qeet, are hot. And some are just not."

Bill's thoughts roamed back to Nialme's body, so alien and yet so perfect, even when she was rolled into that little armored sphere. Then, naturally, he drifted to the memory of her tongue, drying him after the shower. Bill's daydreams were interrupted by Qeet's screech when he rolled into the research lab and smacked into Kimra's foot.

Funny how easily the Nialme memories dissipated in the presence of Kimra and Captain Rane standing before him. Bill licked his lips before smiling at them. Kimra stood, shiny and reflective, her eyes narrowed as if in deep argument, and Captain Rane was openly furious. But, Bill thought, that was nothing new.

"Ladies," he said as he nodded.

"Earth Moron," mumbled the captain. She tossed her red curls over her shoulder and glared at him. For the life of him, Bill could not figure out why Captain Rane hated Earthlings so much, unless it was just him. But what in hell did he do to merit her wrath?

"Bill Griffin," Kimra interjected with a stern look at Sanya. "Captain Rane and I were just discussing our mission. I'm pleased you are conscious and present. We have a task for you. That is, if you will volunteer for it." She glanced at BG and smiled up at him. "I see you have recovered from the hand job I performed while you slept. Well done."

Bill let his mouth fall open. "Hand job? What, did I sleep through that? Are you kidding me?"

"I never 'kid,' Bill Griffin," answered Kimra, reaching out and stroking his prosthetic, as if admiring a work of art.

She held BG for a moment longer than was comfortable for Bill. He let out an embarrassed chuckle, realizing that her 'hand job' comment was actually referring to the newly improved BG 2.0.

Ignoring Bill's response, Kimra continued, "I have completely overhauled your magnificent tool, and it is ready to show you everything it can accomplish. I'll be more than accommodating in demonstrating to you its potential after we've discussed the upcoming mission on Rankor. We will be arriving soon." She took a deep breath and when she exhaled, Bill deliberately leaned in to inhale the entrancing aroma of WD-40.

Not in a million years did Bill ever think he would call the smell of WD-40 entrancing. Space changes a person.

Sanya Rane was visibly and literally biting her tongue. Now she let loose. "Do you *mind*, Human Griffin?"

"Not at all, Captain. But my presence was requested here. Just following orders, trying my best to accommodate your needs. I assume you have needs?"

Rane stared at Bill, silently daring him to keep talking. When he didn't take the bait, she squinted and said, "Fine. Stop talking. While you were *sleeping*, actual *work* was getting done."

Rane turned back to Kimra. "To confirm, we have now entered the Rhapsodic Bohem system and are headed toward the planet Rankor. We have a more complete schematic of the Rankor target, thanks to newly acquired intel from our operative on Little Pekkur. The intel has also given you more leverage in your tasks, I believe. And Ryval is most definitely housed at the target, just as the captured Vlad confessed, Kimra."

"Also, we now know of Blue Balzar's orders to have me, and if possible, my entire tech staff delivered to the Rankodors," said Kimra.

"Thanks to your powers of forceful persuasion, we got lucky on that," said Rane reflectively.

Kimra shuddered, an unusual reaction, as she turned to address Bill. "The Rankodors are even more base than Earth—" She stopped herself. "Ah, baser than most sentient beings. They live solely to function according to their primal instincts. They eat, they eliminate waste, they mate on a constant basis, not even paying attention to bodily cycles, and they eat again. They eat everything, anything, anyone. There is no reliable vocation, no rewarding play. Just Rankodors, existing."

"Whatever, whatever!" Sanya Rane interrupted. "We are well within the boundaries of Rhapsodic Bohem and need to review our plan of action before reaching Rankor orbit."

"Agreed," Kimra said. "The other important piece of information that came from my delicate session with the captured Vlad is that Blue Balzar himself is within striking distance of Rankor. We have very little time once we land on the planet to complete the mission."

"And this mission? Can one of you review that for me and my part in it?" Bill asked.

"Oh. My. Lorde," Rane said with an eye roll. "Let's do this in bite sizes, shall we? Marzz. Ryval Marzz himself is being held prisoner on Rankor. We are charged with freeing him. Before Blue Balzar gets to him. Or gets to us. Both."

"Okay, wow. Thank you, Captain. I can see clearly now," Bill said. "And I've been called here because why? Sorry to be an Earthling, but it usually does circle around to 'where do I come in?' Right?" He gave a little laugh to lighten the mood, but neither woman was moved. Kimra turned and sidled up next to him, like a drunk girl at a prom, and his breath caught for a moment as her metallic arm draped over his shoulder.

But then, before he could even swallow, her other hand reached down to his crotch. At first, adrenaline and delight flooded his body, but then Bill looked down and realized Kimra had a syringe in her hand and by then it was just too late to do anything about the prick in his pants.

He looked at her with a betrayed expression. "What—"

"It's all right, Bill Griffin. Take a breath," Kimra said as she checked the level of serum in her syringe. "This is only an initial test."

"A test for what? Not in the balls again. What the fuck, Kimra?"

"You need to put that word away, Mister Panty Waist," Rane said. "This is my ship, and we use smart words. The 'f' word is not one of them, according to my review of Earth linguistics."

"Excuse me, Captain," Bill said. "But when a woman reaches down in parts I consider private and injects me with heaven knows what, I think that warrants an 'f' word." He made little air quotes for her. "And if you don't, well, you said yourself not long ago that you aren't *my* captain. So, fuck you and the spaceship you rode in on."

That was what he said, or thought he said, or wanted to say. But it didn't come out like that, that last sentence. Instead, it came out as a little "Chirrup!"

He clutched his throat and his eyes got wide, frantically seeking Kimra's comforting look for reassurance that all was well.

"All right, then," said Kimra after a deep breath. "The shift has begun. Look at his armpits." She pointed, and Bill flapped at her hand, only to see in horror that his arm was no longer a human arm, but a fur-feather covered triangle.

Both women peered under the other arm to watch the other half of his torso change.

"Brrrrp! Churrrup! This madness!" Bill started hopping up and down while the women covered their mouths but didn't stifle their amused looks.

"How long do you think this will last?" Sanya Rane absent-mindedly curled a red lock around and around an index finger.

"According to weight indices and metabolic processes, it should be two, maybe three Earth hours. Certainly not longer," Kimra answered. She watched in fascination, inputting information into her device as Bill squawked and shrank down past her hips, then her thighs, finally to stand not even as tall as her silvery knees.

He punched the air in panic and noticed with a start that BG had changed form, too, but was still with him, nonetheless. It fit snuggly on his right wing in a compact and efficient little white triangle. He opened his beak mouth to protest.

"Dammit, I'm. Right here." His voice was high-pitched, barely more than a squeak, but at least words were coming out. "What have you done? Kimra?! Explain, dammit."

"And will he be able to communicate with them? The Rankodors?" Rane reached down idly and chucked Bill under his feathery chin. He gave her hand a mean-spirited peck.

"That would be ideal, yes. The nano-transducer forming in the Broca's area of his brain will ultimately conform to the communicative patterns of whatever species he has become." She nodded appreciatively as Captain Rane murmured her admiration.

"Well, I'm sorry I doubted you, Kimra," Rane said. "Look at the little guy! His crazy baby feet are out now. It's almost done! Aren't you the cutest tiny Earthling ever! I'm not overly fond of Qeet, but this is an improvement over the human."

Qeet had been teleporting from one of the women's shoulders to the next, excitedly babbling and flapping his arms.

"Qeet meet Qeet! Yes?" He teleported to the far side of the research lab and pushed with all his might against a full-length whiteboard. The reverse side of the board was a mirror. "Bill Griffin! Come meet Qeet! Haha Haha!"

Bill started walking, but suddenly found himself in front of the mirror as if by magic. He had no memory of how he had gotten here. He turned in fury to look at the women, and realized they were at the other side of the research lab.

He must have teleported.

He swallowed hard and looked at Qeet beside the mirror. Qeet's eyes were wider than Bill had ever seen them, and the little creature gave him a shrug and a look that could have been horror but could have been delight. And then Bill Griffin looked up.

He saw Qeet hopping up and down. And he saw another Qeet, with BG perched on its wing-arm.

"Chip! Chip! Chip!" Qeet squeaked, hopping and flapping his arms in excitement.

"Arghhhhh!" Bill answered, but it came out as a giant burp squawk. "Fuuuuuuck!"

Chapter 23: Part of the Plan

Qeet was just so happy.

And Bill was so unhappy.

Together, they bounced and squawked and screeched at the mirror, then faced each other and had another round of sounds. Bill batted his arm-wings to knock Qeet away from him, and Qeet squealed in glee, thinking it was a new glorious game.

"I said, *Hey*!" Kimra, hands on hips and bobbling her silver head, finally broke into the noise of it all. "Qeet? Do you need to spend some time in the maze?"

Qeet stopped bouncing and slammed his beak mouth shut.

"And you, sir?" Kimra reached out to grasp BG and yank Bill away from Qeet. Bill's only terrifying thought was that once again the prosthetic would be ripped off, making him pass out again. He, too, shut his beak mouth.

"Now, Bill Qeet Griffin. Let me disseminate the information that you may not have been able to process formerly." Kimra shooed away Captain Rane's teasing hand from under Bill's chin. "You have been injected with a serum, using both deoxyribonucleic acid strands and synthetic sensitizers. Due to the low dosage used, the effects will be temporary."

"Um," squeaked Bill. "What effects?"

"The low-dose chemical compounds will assist in the complete shifting from one living species to another. Again, to emphasize, the effects are temporary."

"You mean DNA," Bill said. He peered again into the mirror, touching his face and watching his Qeet reflection touch its face. He jerked BG away from Kimra and the reflected Qeet did, too. "I so wish. Still sleeping. Or eating. Or anything-ing. Anything but— get *away*, damn you!" He lunged at Qeet, who had stealthily sidled up next to him, and was astounded at BG's response. BG's finger claws extended in an instant and Qeet screeched in pain as the claws dug into his backside.

"Boys, boys, boys," Captain Rane said in a sing-song voice. Bill looked at her and realized she was loving every moment of this crazy turn of events.

Qeet transported away from the painful clutches of BG and Bill looked forlornly at his empty hand, now only flashing soft pastel lights.

Kimra cleared her throat and a waft of WD-40 drifted down into Bill's face.

"While you were sleeping, Bill Griffin, Captain Rane and I have arrived at a blueprint of a plan to rescue Ryval Marzz from the Rankor prison. We will simply shift you, with the assistance of my newest serum, into a Rankodor. You will look and act and think and speak just like the Rankodors. No one will ever suspect you." She gave a tight-lipped metallic smile.

Bill could not find words even if he were still able to speak like a true human. His little beak mouth fell open in dismay, but no words came out.

"You will," Kimra continued, "accompany me to the prison. I will be a hostage, of sorts, and you will be the Rankor hero who has captured me. Once inside the prison, I will locate Ryval Marzz. You, as a Rankodor, and of course Ryval, being Ryval, will find a way to release us both and we will return to the *Tenuous Hope*. How does that sound?" She gave a satisfied look to Sanya, who nodded at her.

"Wait. What?" Bill felt a bit dizzy but held himself up by holding onto the mirror. "That does *not* sound at all. Like plan."

"Well," Captain Rane said with a little snort. "Call it part of the plan, then. We will make sure you're safe, little fuzzbot. We are smart. Trust us. And Ryval is brilliant. Beautiful *and* brilliant. He will fill in the blanks in a way even you can understand." She gave him another annoying chuck under his chin, and he pecked at her hand.

"We thought originally of turning you into a Vlad," Rane said, leaning back on her heels. "All drool and doggy smell and grossness. But then we thought better of it."

Bill looked at Kimra for an explanation. She talked as she worked her tablet. "Yes, it would have given you a bit of an edge, strength-wise, to have taken on the

Vlad form, but we decided it would be less risky for you as well as the mission, as a Rankodor."

Feeling a wave of relief over not having to shift into a Vlad, Bill was reminded of how the *Hope* crew had brutally dispatched the recent Vlad attackers. And he had no desire of becoming Rikki's next meal or any future meal. Or even an appetizer.

Kimra continued, "The Rankodors and Vlads tend not to trust one another, so we are better off using the Rankodor form. Reaching Ryval as a Rankodor is just more feasible, with fewer risks. And we had plenty of cells to work with in the research lab."

Bill felt queasy. He didn't even know what a Rankodor was. Didn't know who Ryval was. Didn't know how to locate the prison. It always came back around, though, to what he would have been if these women had not taken the time to stop on the moon for him. He'd be dead. And really, if Clarity were no longer a living, breathing, perfect woman out there somewhere, what was the difference, if he died as a Rankodor or a Vlad or a Qeet. Or simply Bill Griffin?

He sighed and looked up at Kimra, clutching his talon-paws together in frustration. Suddenly BG lit up like a lighthouse beacon. "How positive are you," he asked in his old Bill Griffin voice, "to what percentage, I mean, that I will not be a Qeet, say, oh I don't know, an hour from now? In order to have time, you know, to acquaint myself perhaps, with who and what a Rankodor is, maybe get a handle, so to speak, on the schematics of the city, locate the prison, etcetera, etcetera, and so forth?"

After a stunned moment, Kimra said, "The human genome contains so many variations that affect distribution, metabolism, and excretion, that it makes things difficult to predict precisely. Part of the reason is because we have such a small sample size to deal with. As you are well aware, we are now very short on human material. To answer your question, affirmative, you will be shifting back to your human form very soon."

She looked down at her tablet and Bill thought her inputting of data was a bit frantic. Her demeanor did not inspire confidence.

"Why can't someone else do this mission of yours, anyway? Someone with strength? Knowledge of who the hell your Ryval character is, maybe? What's wrong with Captain Rane, here, mighty warrior? Warrior-ess?" protested Bill.

Sanya lifted her lip, ready to retort, but Kimra interrupted her. "Actually, we have experimented on several species in the past, since shifting to different creatures, as you can imagine, would be quite valuable in space travel. There are, after all, millions of life forms, not all of which are, shall we say, hospitable? What you would call 'friendly'?"

Bill started to speak but Kimra held up a shiny hand to stop him. "Trust me, Bill Griffin, every being who has stepped foot on the *Hope* has contributed to my body of work, and when it comes to this particular shifting experience, only the human has lasted, er, succeeded at it."

"All in the name of science your brand of persuasion, right, Kimra?" Captain Rane asked.

"Call it what you will, Captain. My experiments, to my thinking, lead to survival. Yours included," Kimra said, still looking at her tablet.

"Wait," Bill said, waving his feathery arms. "Did you experiment on me? To see if I could 'handle it'? One of those times when I was passed out cold?"

"Hmm, yes and no," Kimra answered. "Whereas before we had no conception of whether the shift protocol would work on other species, we did indeed have supporting data that led us to conclude to a high degree of success that human physiology could adapt successfully to shifting."

"What the fuck is a 'high degree'? Are you saying you *guessed*, or excuse me, you *hypothesized* that your mysterious 'protocol' would work on me?" Bill bounced up onto Kimra's examination table in his fury and looked her right in the eyes.

"I calculated, Bill Griffin," Kimra said with a maddening calm, "the probabilities of success based on previous experiments and actions. Today's serum is formulated purely on solid scientific study and observations." She waved her hand and a screen came forward from the research lab wall. "As you can see from my extensive research, logical predictions were tested and summarily discounted if not proven true; empirical evidence was held fast and re-tested, and when new consequences made themselves evident, well. I'm sure you can see the clarity of this basic scientific process."

"Yes, I'm sure I see the Clar—"

Qeet had transported to face Bill upside down, his little wing arms flapping to keep them nose to nose. He reached out almost tenderly, grasped Bill's earlobes and pulled himself closer.

"Bill Griffin is Qeet, too. Qeet loves Mr. Bill. We are Qeet family, now."

"Qeet," Bill said after taking a deep breath, "You been watching those old Earth vids in the K-torium?"

"Bill watch with Qeet soon?" Qeet batted his eyes, and Bill had a sudden thought. He gently pushed the little monkey bird aside.

"Indeed, my little friend." Bill smiled, as much as his little beak mouth would allow.

And then he turned and half-walked, half-fluttered away.

Bill could feel Sanya Rane's eyes drilling a hole in the back of his head as he stormed off. He heard her click her teeth and mutter ever so quietly, "What the fuck?"

Chapter 24: Ooh, That Smell

After a bit of experimenting with the controls in the K-torium, Bill found himself pacing and weaving between life-sized images of the love of his life, Clarity Thomas. Clarity in high school, Clarity wearing a proud grin in her new cadet suit, Clarity boarding the *Eleanor Gaye*, ready for her most recent mission. Bill remembered how proud Clarity was to have been asked to name her ship.

Hearing Qeet and the others approaching the K-torium, Bill quickly changed the images, like a teenager hiding his porn mags so as not to get caught red-handed by his parents, or worse, a grandmother.

As Qeet, Kimra, and Rane entered the chamber, Bill looked up at the image to see an innocuous babbly brook coursing through a green meadow. He winced at the screen-cover choice. So much for not being obvious.

"Seems like the *Tenuous Hope's* database is really as detailed and extensive as the galaxy," Bill said in a hushed voice. It was his human voice, but he was still in Qeet form. "You mentioned the clarity of your scientific method earlier, Kimra. Then Qeet mentioned watching vids. I got curious and a touch homesick. Wanted to see if you had more information in the database, perhaps about other humans." He attempted to swallow.

"Fortunately for us, and particularly for you, Bill Griffin," said Kimra, "we were able to download Earth's entire historical archive before it was destroyed. There will be more opportunities for you to explore the database later, I can assure you." Kimra waved her hand and the image of the brook disappeared. "You can see images of your friend, and maybe even read about her when we return with Ryval Marzz. You haven't read anything yet? About your Earthling friend?" Another tight smile.

"No," said Bill. "I was just getting started. Please," he said, taking Kimra's face between his little triangle wings, "please let me do just a little research while I de-Qeet?"

"I'm afraid this needs to be what you Earthlings call delayed gratification, Bill," said Rane. "We're a little thrown off by your ability to teleport like you just did. Kimra, do you have any new findings?"

Kimra checked her tablet and input something. "Yes, it is a mystery. Normally, we would expect a shift to exhibit only the physicality of the mimicked organism, without any of that creature's innate powers or abilities. The fact that you teleported raises important questions as it relates to your upcoming shift to Rankodor form. Have a seat." She motioned toward a bench and Bill dejectedly perched as only Qeets can perch.

"Not convinced Rane believes I'm needed," he said.

"You are the only damn human on board, Moron! Stop arguing! Blue Balzar wants us dead, and we need Ryval and all his new intel in order to escape that end. Only humans can survive the serum to shift temporarily. You get all that? For the third time?" Captain Rane's skin flushed a deep emerald green as she leaned toward him.

"Yes," Kimra said gently as she took Sanya's hand and deftly moved her away from Bill. "Unfortunately, what it comes down to is *you*. You are our only hope, Bill Griffin." Her eyes widened almost unperceptively, but Bill felt what it was she was seeing.

He felt it in his groin, in his head, and in BG. He was shifting back to human form. He looked down and sure enough, the white feather fur was gone, replaced with a goose-bumped arm. Realizing he was most likely going to shift naked, Bill groaned and prepared to cover the parts he could.

Kimra stood transfixed, lost in thought as he shifted. Bill saw Sanya Rane out of the corner of his eye, her gaze frozen on his crotch.

"Hey! Show's over!" he shouted at her and she turned her back.

"Oh, please," she said. "As if. I was merely thinking that you're shifting a bit, uh, prematurely, if you will. You should be, um, lasting longer. Right, Kimra?"

Kimra nodded. "Unfortunately, the Captain is correct, Bill. This means the serum needs to have a significant boost in potency if we are going to complete the mission with you in Rankodor form."

"Right," Rane said. "Can't have you go total Earthling while you are in the thick of it."

"Given what we have observed so far, perhaps an enhanced formulation will pull him through the entirety of the mission as a Rankodor," Kimra said. "I surmise that acquiring the Qeet teleport power has burned through the serum more quickly. No matter," she said, making a little tsking sound with her lips and turning to the center stage of the K-torium.

"We will see to it that you manage on Rankor." She snapped her fingers and the lights went low. "Let us run through a summation of what we know, what you should know, what we need to know."

Bill cleared his throat and looked down at his now completely human and completely naked body. "Hey, not to stop this show before it begins, but some clothes would be a nice touch, maybe?"

Suddenly, his suit came bobbing toward him through the air, and he realized Qeet had beaten him to the realization. When the clothes dumped over Bill's feet, a fluffed-up Qeet remained hanging in mid-air, his eyelids at half-mast.

"Thanks, Qeet," Bill said. "Hey, you okay?" Qeet seemed to have lost all of his energy.

"Qeet sad, Bill Griffin." Qeet parked himself inconveniently in Bill's naked lap. "Qeet felt like home, like Bill Griffin, Qeet was family." His little clawed feet flexed dangerously close to what Aunt Em used to jokingly call the 'family jewels'.

Bill winced and gently moved Qeet to the floor. "We can still be family, even if we don't look alike," he said. "For now, though, I'd appreciate just an iota of privacy while I slip into something less uncomfortable. Ladies?"

"Oh, for galaxy's sake," Sanya Rane said, rolling her eyes. She turned and followed Kimra out into the corridor while Bill dressed. When he stepped out of the chamber fully clothed, there was quite a crowd waiting at the threshold.

He saw Surrep's breasts first, of course. Hard not to notice eight perfect orbs bouncing around, barely concealed under the vest. Behind her was a flash of blue, and Bill assumed it was the Octo woman, Cali. The ship's crew was there in full force, noticeably uncomfortable, shifting on their feet, not talking to each other.

Nialme rolled in and unfurled. She looked at him with soulful eyes and embraced him, long and warm and deep. She reached out for a trembling Qeet, tucked him tightly to her torso, rolled up again, and careened down the corridor without a word.

"What the—" Bill watched her go but was distracted when a fully vertical Rikki sashayed into the room, sleek and sexy and apparently recovered from her food coma.

"Sssee you, fingers crosssed, Bill Griffin," she said, and she took his face tenderly between her yellow and brown patterned hands and slipped her skinny long tongue into his mouth before Bill could even get a grip on himself. He felt his stomach sink to his knees.

"Glad to know you ate recently, Rikki," Bill stuttered. He looked at Kimra then Rane and asked,

"What's going on, here? Why do I feel like I'm going on a one-way trip to hell?"

"Tssst," said Rikki. "We jussst know you leave for a scary mission on a scary planet with very sssmelly creatures who get sadissstic sometimes."

"Ahhhh, okay, then," said Bill. "How's about we start that show you had planned, there, Kimra? Maybe I need to see what I'm about to go up against?"

"Oh, bad choice of words, Earthling," Captain Rane said. "You get 'up against' one of these things, and you will be blubbering for your mama, as they say." She gave a bark of a laugh and flipped her red hair back.

Bill squinted at her. Just about the only thing he liked about this woman was that hair. That hair seemed so familiar, coppery and soft and long, and perfectly curled.

His thoughts were interrupted by the lights dimming once again. Rikki and Surrep, her breasts flapping for all the world to see, and Cali the octomom, made themselves at home on the bench seats behind Kimra, Captain Rane, and Bill.

Before them, and sitting on benches beside them, and turning slowly like those women in the Earthling olden days who sold transport vehicles in showrooms, circling around to display every angle of themselves, were strange tufted creatures.

None of the creatures stood more than five feet tall, and their brown shaggy hair sprouted from their shoulders, their asses, their feet and from the tips of their stiff little nubbly naked stalks of tails. The tails reminded Bill of wet lollipops that had rolled around some seriously neglected under-the-bed dust bunnies.

The Rankodor faces, seen from these incredible three-dimensional holograms, were terrifying muzzles, angry-looking and revealing oversized orange teeth that had obvious decay issues. Good dental hygiene did not appear to be a priority on Rankor.

"These are representative samples of the planet's populace," Kimra began. "As you can see, Rankodors appear to be quite uniform, not unlike our Qeet and his ilk. The male Rankodor and female Rankodor look identical, and in fact, depending upon circumstances, Rankodors can easily switch genders in order to mate with one another."

"Oh, dear," said Surrep, wiping her top breasts. "I have never! Well, I mean, I have never, yet."

Kimra cleared her throat and said, "Absolutely, Surrep, no judgements here."

Bill inhaled, resigned to whatever fate awaited on Rankor, and Kimra continued. "From our collective experience and from what we have gleaned from prisoners and informants, the Rankodors have little or no regard to time management or what actions they might conceive as work. When Rankodors are hungry, they will abandon any mission or any other responsibility to eat. Likewise, with thirst, essentially Rankodors drink when thirsty, roadblocks be damned.

"When sexual thoughts enter the Rankodor mind, he or she will drop everything to engage in whatever kind of mating is readily available, including, as I have previously mentioned, switching genders. A tired

Rankodor never becomes exhausted, because it will simply collapse wherever it may be to nap or sink into longer sleep. Urges of any sort are not ignored."

Kimra raised her hand in a scrolling motion, moving the images along through the presentation. "Because of these attributes," she went on, "the Rankodors are highly unpredictable. One never knows the bodily needs, desires, or rhythms that are coursing through this species, and thus we have difficulty in forming the perfect plan."

"Exactly," said Captain Rane. "We cannot assume that at any given time, the majority of them will be sleeping, or vulnerable to attack or espionage. Because the little varmints just do whatever the heck they want, whenever they want."

"What in hell?" Bill looked right then left. "What is that smell, for crying out loud?"

"That," Kimra said, going back a few images with a reverse scrolling motion, "is the natural odor that you will encounter on Rankor. In fact, that is how you yourself will smell. I just wanted you to become familiar with it; my last scroll should have dissipated it some. Apologies, all."

"Gaaah," exclaimed Bill, waving BG through the air. "It's like if you expressed a dog's anal glands, rolled it over a two-week old skunk corpse, then vomited into the pot. Yikes." He noticed, though, that even as he spoke, BG was fanning through the rank odor and eradicating it quite efficiently.

"Bathing on Rankor," Kimra said, "is not employed for hygienic purposes. Although rumor has it,

Rankodors do have cleansing machines on their planet. The creatures base their level of attraction or attack on the odors of others. Don't assume, however, that odors are the necessary component to either of those activities; again, a Rankodor will react to another for any variety of reasons. The odor just magnifies their pleasure in the activity they choose to pursue."

"What do they actually *do* on this miserable rock, anyway?" Bill asked. "I mean, how do they get their supplies? Their food?"

"All good questions, Bill Griffin."

Kimra scrolled again and Bill watched the holograms in fascination. Some Rankodors fell over to sleep, most were vacuuming disgusting food into their mouths, and others started humping each other, or at least it looked like humping. Maybe it was fighting.

"As you can see, our database has only so much information, most of which I have already divulged. It could be that Rankor is a trading hub of sorts, since they do not seem to ever be at a loss for food. They certainly have shown that no mission or job, if you will, is more imperative than bodily needs. And furthermore," Kimra said, holding up an index finger and pointing to a fire burning right behind a couple of what appeared to be mating Rankodors, "once any desired activity is begun, nothing, and I mean nothing, gets the slightest attention until that particular need is fulfilled. The only things they actually finish on Rankor are meals, sleep sessions, and intercourse."

"Actually, sounds like some of my friends back home," Bill said with a sadness in his voice.

"Unlike your friends, though, you must go out of your way, Bill, to avoid touching a Rankodor. Not even in casual passing. Any physical contact is an invitation to engage, whether that engagement is intimacy or conflict. This law of the species is universal across gender and age. Do not touch. Is that clear?"

"Pretty sure I just described their stink as a mix of skunk, vomit, and dog butt with a little bit of death mixed in," Bill said, scratching the back of his neck. "So, yep, understood. Crystal clear. No touchy, no problem."

"I have other concerns, Bill Griffin," said Kimra, cocking her head. "For the sake of research, we need to know how you physically reacted to the Qeet shift. For instance, did you feel that you were entirely in control of your body while you were a Qeet?"

"Not really a very smart question," Bill answered. "I was a fucking Qeet, right?" He ignored the offended grunt that came from Captain Rane. "I mean, if I had been in control, I would have shifted back to, well, me."

"Understood, of course. What I meant was, did you understand the workings of your own brain while you were shifted? Did you have a full grasp of who you actually were, a Qeet shifted from a human? Or did you feel like a Qeet?"

"Absolutely. I knew I was Bill Griffin, and I heard her name, that is, I was reminded of something and remembered how to get here, to the K-torium, and I recognized..." His eyes got a little glassy at the thought of Clarity again, but he shook his head. "And Qeet was annoying me. So, I obviously wasn't welcoming his play as a fellow Qeet. Why? What would the difference be?"

"Well, duh!" Rane stood up, staring at him like he was mentally challenged. "If you shifted into a Rankodor and then were skipping around down there, you might just end up getting porked by another Rankodor! As in, 'bad things happen to dudes in prison.' How many fingers do I have up?" She put her hand up with three fingers.

"Look, Captain. I'm not stupid. I'm just not as familiar with changing into a member of another species, and furthermore, I'm pretty sure that if you were in my place, you'd ask some basic questions, too. So, lay off!"

Ten's voice wafted through the room, drawing everyone's attention. "Captain Sanya Rane, we are approaching Rankor. Captain Rane?"

She glared at Bill. "We have very little time for you to get your act together, PeeWee Griffin. We will be launching the *Vestige* shortly." She nodded at Kimra and stormed from the K-torium, hair flying.

"The *Vestige*?"

"Yes," Kimra said. "The *Last Vestige*. She is our pod, our shuttle. It will be easier and more efficient for us to transport to Rankor without endangering the rest on board. The ship will stay a fair distance away, hidden, but in orbit."

Kimra motioned for Bill to follow her out into the hall and they made their way silently back to the research lab.

"Because your Qeet transformation lasted such a short time," Kimra explained, "I will design this serum to be just a bit stronger. Based on your physiological reaction, we should see you as a Rankodor for at least a blitz." She worked methodically behind her station, mixing and examining a variety of berry-colored potions that were graphically represented on the display.

"A blitz?"

"Apologies, approximately three of your Earth hours." She looked up at him as she prepared a syringe. Her eyes softened for a moment. "You will be fine, Bill Griffin. Trust me. Now, this will not hurt a bit." She drew her injection back, giving him a confident smile.

Before he had time to react, she injected him in his nether regions.

"Ack!" he exclaimed. "Again with the balls?"

"Oh, my sincere apologies," Kimra said with feigned concern. "Force of habit now, I guess."

Bill thought he detected a hint of a smirk on Kimra's metallic face. He shrugged and just shook his head. "Oh, Kimra. Fool me thrice."

Chapter 25: Feel Like a Number

Standing before the mirror that had already betrayed him once, Bill was, not unexpectedly, horrified to watch his body slowly shift into a Rankodor. He was held spellbound nonetheless, witnessing the fascinating transformation. BG was first to change as its length shortened and sprouted light brown fuzz all over its surface.

Almost losing his balance, Bill's right leg began shrinking in length, while growing in girth. The other leg soon followed a similar metamorphosis.

Kimra helped him out of his skin suit with full Kimra efficiency just as a nubby naked tail popped out of his butt, complete with a poodle-esq brown pompom on the end. The excitement of Kimra undressing him, augmented by the physical primal sexual instincts of the Rankodor species, caused Bill's male Rankodor member to stand at full attention, which was surprisingly statuesque.

"Oh my!" exclaimed Kimra, as she caught a glimpse of Bill's standing ovation.

Bill's body was still in different stages of Earthling-to-Rankodor change, but he was relieved to see red-brown body hair, or more like fur, growing longer and thicker in quick fashion, especially over his raging erection.

"Best not to destroy too many of these garments," Kimra murmured to herself with a conspiratorial smile at Bill, ignoring his momentary embarrassment.

He couldn't even come up with a snide remark, as his full attention was now on mentally suppressing his sexual urges. He concentrated on examining the shape of his body, never perfect in human form, but now melding into a pear shape, almost kiwi-birdish. His mouth dried as he watched tufts of brown hair spurt from his shoulders and back. A muzzle had poked out from his face, hairless and wrinkled.

Kimra busied herself behind him like a mother helping prep her daughter for prom. She waited while BG became a claw-like hand, then strapped blue and green cuffs around his new wrists.

"What are these for?" he asked, licking his lips, and desperately wishing for spit.

"The Rankodors love to show off their collections of cuffs and cufflinks to each other," she said, threading the links through the holes in the cuffs. His were little Earths, stones of blue and green with white wisps running around them. His breath caught, and for a moment Bill thought he might be tearing up.

"These will help us know it's you, you see," said Kimra. "Most of these smelly organisms appear to be cut from the same mold. Except for their cuffs and their links, we have trouble discerning who's who, if you will. At least from my research so far. Whew!" She waved her graceful metallic arm through the air. "Goodness, Bill Griffin! What did you have for lunch?"

Now that she mentioned it, the room had taken on a new and god-awful odor. Definitely corpse-ish. Like when he would go hiking on Earth and know immediately there was a dead deer or raccoon in the woods.

"Step in," Kimra said. She had put an odor-mask over her face and now offered up a brown tunic that he stepped into, sort of like overalls back home, but with only one strap over the right shoulder and no pant legs. There were pockets on the apron part of the overall, and others down the sides. All of the pockets were bulging.

"What's in here?" Bill asked, leaning on Kimra as he adjusted his footing. She gagged a little and Bill realized he had been talking over her shoulder and his breath was causing the gag. He jerked up to peer into the mirror and shrank from the face before him. Cheesy-poof-sized orange teeth hung from his lipless mouth, and all of them had black holes of rot.

Bill closed his eyes as he felt his throat tighten, then loosen. When next he spoke, his voice was gravelly, as if he had a bad cold and couldn't clear his throat, like mucous was gumming up his pronunciation. "In the pogets. Whas in the pogets?"

Kimra stepped back and Bill could tell she was trying really hard to smile kindly behind that mask.

"Those are photographs. From Earth that I pulled from the archive. They are very, very valuable on Rankor. We believe, again with only limited data resources, that there must be a significant amount of trade on Rankor in order for it to remain in existence. Since everything on Rankor is in constant danger of abandonment in exchange for bodily functions, there is some certainty on our part that the major industry is tourism and trade. We know from one informant that photographs did wonders when it came to her mining information and her ultimate escape."

"Photographs?" Bill's heart leapt. BG went wild with color and he instantly started to claw his pockets, but Kimra stopped him.

"Bill Griffin."

"Wha?" Strange, Bill thought. The mucous was still there, but as it snaked down his throat, he found he actually kind of liked the taste and the feel of it.

"You will need a name down there."

"Ah, 'kay."

"It should not be a problem. The Rankodors have limited imagination and most have opted to name their children with common Rankodor names, like SewerSludge, CessPool, FootRot, PondSlime. You get the picture?"

"Wha? Howa tell ea' otha apart if same nam?" sputtered Bill.

"It is usually sufficient to recite parental names in smaller groups. Only when dealing with large crowds would it be necessary to go back further in lineage," answered Kimra. "Your name is Ralf of Badodor and RottenEggs."

Kimra pulled out handcuffs from a slat in the lab wall with one hand while the other was tightly clamped over her mask. The smell must be getting unbearable.

"Ah. Ralf, then." Bill said, with what he thought was confidence. Yes, in fact. He was completely confident. An empowering new and wonderful feeling. He hocked up a respectable loogy, spat it onto the lab floor, and announced clearly, "That was the name of my grandmother's dog back in the day. A little rescue mutt, I believe."

A Floomba quietly emerged from a hidden slot on the floor. It zoomed over to the impressive glob of brown sputum and slurped it up before disappearing back into its cubbyhole.

Ignoring the vulgar display of etiquette, Kimra said, "Very well, then. Remember that. You are Ralf of Badodor and RottenEggs for the next blitz."

"Blitz, of course. A hundred and eighty Earth minutes."

"That is correct. Now help me," Kimra said.

A faint vibration and humming sound emitted from beyond the walls of the lab on the starboard side of the *Hope*. "That is the *Last Vestige* powering up. We will be on our way once you get these shackles on me. I am your prisoner, remember."

"Yup." Bill deftly locked the cuffs around her silver wrists, then just because he felt like it, ran his hands up and down her body, over her breasts, stopping on her ass. He thrust his crotch toward her and groaned.

"Bill Griffin! Come to your senses immediately!" Kimra slipped out of the handcuffs and put her hands out to ward him away.

"Hey! How'd do tha?"

"They are faux cuffs, Ralf. Just in case of emergency, we need the ability to escape quickly. Now take a deep breath and hold it please. Gaa." She made another gagging sound but stripped off her mask and held out the cuffs for him to again snap over her wrists. "You have to drag me by my hair," she said, quite matter-of-factly.

"Drag you by hair? Ha! Fine!" He grabbed her by her tinseled, color-changing locks that were tied so nicely in a bun. With a gleeful tug he knocked her to the ground and started to stride out of the research lab like a conquering caveman.

"Not now, Bill Griffin! Stop!" Kimra looked up at him when he dropped her head onto the floor. "Honestly! I meant when we disembark from the *Vestige*. On Rankor. So that I will actually appear to be your prisoner."

"Argh. Sorry." Bill leaned over and tried to be chivalrous by helping Kimra stand again. But something just came over him, a whim, a fancy, an erection, tenting his overalls and making the phlegm in the back of his throat even thicker.

"Well, try to contain yourself for the next few minutes, Bill Griffin," Kimra said. She watched and listened to his tortured thinking, all the while backing off. "Okay, now listen, Bill Griffin, and listen good." She straightened up and clamped a hand over her face again. "You are walking now, down that corridor. You are taking the third right. And there you will stop. And wait. For me. Got it?"

"Ghaa. Yesh." Bill felt horrible and lusty and crazy all at once. But he followed instructions. Down the hallway, third right, stop. The hatch to the *Vestige* was open, with only one crew member at the helm. When she smelled him, she looked up in horror and slapped her hands over her nose.

Is it really all that bad? he tossed out there, trying with all his might to maintain some decorum of humanity and decency.

A collective *yes* answered him, some in soft voices, some in anger, one with too many esses. He took a seat on the *Vestige* as far away from the pilot as possible.

"You were supposed to wait, but oh well," Kimra said as she boarded. She placed herself next to the pilot at the helm, breathing into her elbow. "Secure the hatch and engage the drive," she said, and the shuttle's hatch slammed shut.

It was a short trip to Rankor, made all the faster, Bill thought with some level of pride mixed with chagrin, by the pilot's urgency to get him and his odor out the door. Once docked, he excitedly grasped Kimra's arms, putting the trick shackles on her again. Then he grabbed her shiny hair and threw her to the ground.

No more practice, this is the real deal. I am Ralf of Badodor and RottenEggs.

Kimra grimaced up at him and rolled her eyes.

He dragged her struggling body along the dock toward the entrance where a Rankodor dockmaster was stationed.

"Ralf," he said when he reached the end of the docking gate. After the Qeet transformation fiasco, Bill had memorized the schematics that they'd picked up during their stop on Little Pekkur, so he knew exactly which turns to make to find the galactic prison hold.

Seeing Kimra obviously excited the Rankodors' sensibilities, as a few of them approached and gathered around the spectacle.

As if they had planned it, though, they all used prodding sticks instead of their hands to touch her. The sticks looked like the kind of long forks Bill's grandmother had in her garage. Humans used to sit around intentional fires, holding prongs like these with tubes of meat and marshmallows stuck to them. Bill grasped onto this fading memory, fighting the urge to fling himself onto Kimra's exquisite body. He wanted to drink in the smell of her, lounge on top of her while she writhed against him in disgust.

He sucked in to clear his mouth of excess saliva and concentrated on just getting to his destination.

The prison was nothing more than a warehouse, really. A warehouse that resembled an antiquated indoor zoo. After passing through a heavy main gate from the outside corridor, the cell station's ceilings loomed twenty feet high, and the individual cells were deep and dark. Bill, aka Ralf, was waved through as if the Rankodors saw beautiful metallic women being dragged by their hair every day of the summer.

Finally, Bill found himself in front of an empty cell with a custodian waiting at its gate. The custodian's arms were decorated with shiny golden cuffs with little black stars as cufflinks.

"Drop off from Little Pekkur?" the custodian asked.

"Sure. Where's Balzar?" Bill looked over the custodian's shoulder as if expecting the evil blue man to be there in person. "I'm eggspectorating a bounty for this one." He yanked Kimra's hair and dragged her into the cell. The custodian pretended to help him, poking Kimra with his funny stick.

Kimra's eyes had been closed until they reached the cell, but now Bill followed her gaze into the darkness of the cell next to hers. A beautiful specimen of a man clung to the bars of his cell. Bill watched in fascination as the man's muscles rippled and sweat slicked his tanned skin. Why he was shirtless, Bill did not know. Sweet drops of perspiration dripped from his sandy hair. He had a strong cleft chin and a Roman nose, a jaw that clenched above high cheekbones, and eyes that would not leave Kimra's stare.

Bill looked down in wonder at his new erection. "Gah," he said, batting at it and feeling perfectly natural in doing so.

The custodian uttered a chortling kind of sound.

"Good, right? The both."

"Oh yup," Bill said, making a show of holding his crotch. The two Rankodors threw their heads back and guffawed together like they were fraternity brothers at a topless bar.

"Schtick?" asked the custodian.

"Schtick?" Bill answered. The custodian produced a prodding stick just like his own and presented it to Bill. Bill bowed in thanks, and confidently walked back the way he came, never giving Kimra even a backward glance. For reasons he didn't even care to know, he was sure of where he was heading, sure of a good time, and sure he was very, very hungry.

Oh, the music that met his ears once he left the prison behind and followed his nose and some wisp of memorized schematics to the Hall of Quandary. He sucked up saliva again, smelling pond scum or some such delicacy. The music enveloped him, and he paused after entering just to breathe in the atmosphere with an appreciative spirit.

Rankodors danced on tabletops, fucked on the stage, sucked in food and drinks, belched and pissed, and tore at each other in rage. There was blood and vomit and all kinds of bodily fluids on the floor, on the gaming tables, and at the bar. The myriad smells and liquids mixed together in a stinky tantalizing stew.

It felt just like home. Not his physical Earth home. Just the feeling of home.

Bill watched as a Rankodor knocked over a mug while dancing on top of a table. He shuffled forward and picked up the used, slimy mug that had tipped over onto the floor and headed over to an open barrel by the bar. The barrel was about three-quarters full of what looked like actual pond scum, complete with a floating, greenish top layer of slime.

He dipped the mug into the verminous fluid, filling it to the brim. In as few gulps as he could manage, he emptied the mug in two seconds flat. Wiping his mouth with the fur of his forearm, he let out a resounding belch in satisfaction.

As per Rankodor custom, the others let out a chorus of belching in response to show their appreciation of the libations.

Having satiated his need for a drink, Bill stole a moment to take in the chaotic rhythm of the music. He made an involuntary little twitch before starting to dance, but it wasn't any kind of dance he had ever danced before. He flung himself right then forward, twirled like a little girl trying to make herself dizzy, then threw himself down onto the ground amidst all the spills.

Like a turtle stuck on its back, he wriggled his limbs, while all around him Rankodors doused him with some odiferous cocktail, chanting, "Roach! Roach! Roach!" They laughed and he laughed right back at them. With them.

Bill lost himself for several manic minutes, heady with the pounding music, doused in stinky beverages, one of the main attractions in the club. But just as suddenly as it started, the dance ended with the almost subconscious thought of food.

He stood and gave his matted fur a bit of a squeegee, and clapped his hands over his head, all the while turning and scanning the place for a server. When he met eyes with another Rankodor from across the club, he flashed his open palms, then flexed his digits several times. A few more claps and that did it.

He scurried to an open trough and tapped his giant feet impatiently. He was quite sure his stomach was growling, even though it would have been impossible to have heard.

He waited at the trough, feeling initial waves of anger break over him, but the rage didn't last long. Apparently Rankodor cuisine was prepared in bulk and ready to serve with little or no notice.

The server, wearing black and white cuffs with red cufflinks, very smart, marched up to Bill's trough with a wet doughy slab of some kind of bread, along with several small buckets filled with different colored glop. Chunky, gooey glop. Pure heaven.

Bill was delighted. He reached with natural ease into his tunic and pulled out a wad of what Kimra had called *photographs*. Turned out, they were folded pages of old Earth magazines, not actual snapshots like he had seen in the museums back home.

He paid the waiter with a page from a sports magazine, which was confusing, because instead of a human playing ball, the page showed a completely nude woman who had been painted head to toe in various colors of geometric shapes. She sprawled on her stomach as an ocean wave bore down in the background.

After getting momentarily stalled on the naked human girl, Bill clapped several times to let the server know they'd done well, and immediately leaned over his glop, opened his mouth, and breathed in. The sound that emanated from his internal organs was not unlike a vacuum, and his eyes watered in glee as orange, brown, and yellow glop fairly flew into his gaping, toothy mouth, but there was no chewing. Everything just whisked its way up and into the open hole in his face and went down like his mouth was an old-fashioned garbage disposal.

When the glop was gone, Bill ripped the spongy bread into pieces and stuffed his cheeks with it. Better to savor if it's just waiting inside the mouth, ready to go down at a moment's heads up.

With enormous concentration, Ralf opened his mouth, still stuffed with wet globs, and belched long and loud. He even said his name as he belched, knowing somehow that this was a favored trick on Rankor, a talent not all Rankodors could boast.

"Raaalf of Baaadodooor aaaand RottenEgggggsss." He looked around and put a modest hand up in the air as some Rankodors rapped their schticks in appreciation.

Settling in with his newly full stomach, Bill surveyed the room. Rankodors were pairing up and wrestling each other using various strange holds. It became apparent to him why Rankodors wore tunics with no pants as some of the strange holds included grabbing at each other's genitals. Most of the paired agitators got ushered out of the main hall and into separate rooms once things heated up. Red and green flashing lights perched above the doorways to the private rooms, perhaps a control for the bouncer types to know which were occupied and which weren't.

Bill swung away from his trough and his prodding schtick got caught up in a passing Rankodor's decorative cuffs. Bill gave the schtick a nice fishing-rod kind of yank, and gasped when he realized he'd snagged the entire cuff, a classic black and white zebra stripes. He brought it up to his eyes, stunned and strangely excited all at once, and then he realized that the Rankodor he had just accidentally pickpocketed stood before him now, scratching at itself in irritation.

"Sorry," Bill said, thinking his lips might be curling in a smile, but not quite sure if that smile might instead look like a threatening flash of fangs. The mucous strands in the back of his throat had dissipated after eating, and he realized he was able to speak more clearly now. "Seems like I hooked you by accident!"

The other Rankodor didn't seem amused. Its muzzle mouth opened and closed like a nervous guppy. Brown glop dripped from its teeth.

Bill smiled again. Or tried to. "Here you go, no hard feelings," he said, as he delicately wrapped the black and white cuff around the Rankodor's wrist, patting it when it was buttoned up nice and neat with its red stone of a link.

The Rankodor's eyes widened and its mouth froze in its open position and Bill knew in that instant that he had just made what was most likely a critical error in judgement.

The Rankodor's stare went from Bill's eyes down to where his hands were still resting on the cuffs, then slowly back to Bill's face.

"Fester of PondScum and MaggotMeal," it said. "Who you?"

"I'm Bill, I mean Ralf," Bill said. "Ralf of Badodor and RottenEggs, that is." BG was getting strangely slippery.

"Ah. Your name sound familiar. I have eaten. You?"

"What? Oh, yes, yeah, I ate. Delish, right?" Bill started to take back his hand, but the Rankodor caught it in his and pulled Bill close.

"You have challenged me, Ralf. Get a room."

"Oh, get a room? This is what I get for having been out of town so long," Bill said. "I'd love to, but you see, I just brought a prisoner in from, uh, way out there, and I need to stay close so—"

"Get. A. Room," demanded Fester. It reached out for Bill's prodding schtick and caressed it, a weird absent-minded look on his face. Her face? Bill realized as he looked around the room that all the Rankodors were involved in some semblance of struggle or maybe dance.

Watching the shuffle of his feet following the Fester dude or chick, he understood that he was being guided into a private room. He looked at Rankodor faces as they passed. Some looked like they could be enjoying some kind of foreplay. Others looked like they were on the verge of amputating their sparring partner's appendages.

"Clusterfuck," he muttered to himself.

Chapter 26: Make Me Wanna Shoop

The bouncer Rankodor yanked both of their schticks out of their hands, flipped the internal switch, and changed their light to red. The door slammed behind them. Bill put his hands before him beseechingly and tried again.

"Crazy but true, I really just lost track of my manners, it seems—"

"No." Fester pressed itself against the door and took very deep, fast breaths. There were green stringy things stuck in its orange teeth, and its eyes were rolled into the back of its head.

And suddenly, it pushed itself off the door and sprinted across the room, squashing Bill against the far wall. They both grunted with the impact, as Bill felt his lungs collapse. His release of air sounded like a growl.

The Rankodor growled back, and its mouth flew open with a snapping sound, like the sound of a combination lock coming undone. Bill snapped his mouth open in an involuntary response, and it, too, locked in a wide-open position, his teeth dripping with the leftovers of his delicious lunchtime stew.

They bounced off of each other like super balls, Fester slamming against the adjacent wall, only to bound back and smack into Bill's body again. Bill thought of little, but his mind was a slideshow of mental images, a late Sunday afternoon Earth vid of battering elk antlers in a snowy forest, then thick-furred grizzlies by a raging river, yelling at each other in foul-mouthed bear tongue.

He joined the cacophony in his mind and in this fuming room, ranting in a Rankodor accent at this total stranger who might be out to kill him.

Bill Griffin was in heaven. His heart pounded as they bounced and squashed, slammed and yowled at each other. He knew all the steps as if he'd spent the week rehearsing a finely tuned choreography, sidling along the wall only to crush his opponent, then bouncing away to spin and tangle his arms and legs with good old Fester.

Green gunk oozed from their noses and their breath came in rasps, but still they slammed and squirmed against each other, sometimes grabbing the other's neck with dripping teeth and shaking their heads furiously.

The air was musky, and Bill noticed the sweat dripping off their bodies wasn't just regular sweat; it was greasier, milky and pungent, and it poured from every inch of him like a lubricant. When he noticed it, he stopped for a moment to remark about it.

"Whew! Look at this shit, will you?" He shook his left arm, BG alight and blazing, and watched as enormous droplets dribbled onto the floor.

It's a defense mechanism, meant to make it difficult for one's enemy to subdue you. Watch, watch!

He barely had time to realize that he still had a glimmer of live communications with his shipmates. Bill shook his head a bit in recognition. He needed to pay attention to his mission. He needed to get control. He needed to find Clarity, get revenge for Earth's destr—

Too late, he saw the Rankodor leaning down in an almost comical bow before him, dipping its fingers into the little puddle of sweat that had stopped Bill in the first place. The Rankodor stood and slowly, almost seductively, drew its fingers into its mouth, slurping loudly and with obvious satisfaction. It bared its fuzzy teeth at Bill and froze.

"There, now, Fester," Bill said, and he cleared his throat, because now the mucous was once again starting to thicken into strands. "Perhaps we could just stop and talk this one out? I don't know about you, but whew! I'm winded!"

Fester looked different, all of a sudden. There was a softness to its stare. The hard lines around its mouth were gone. It leaned in toward Bill and inhaled a long, luxuriant breath and began to circle Bill. Its feet crossed then separated, crossed then separated. Bill thought about an old ritualistic Greek wedding he had been to back home. All they needed were some hankies.

The Rankodor closed in, but Bill had by now gotten lost in the moment. The glory of Rankor, he thought, as his eyes rolled back into his head, is what matters right here. Right now. Needing, then filling the need. Over and over again.

His feet started mirroring his partner's, crossing, stepping forward, then back, and then they were together, smearing their goo all over each other, dripping and grunting and howling, until at last they stopped the vertical dance to fall on each other.

The Rankodor spun like a top on Bill's body, ripping at Bill's tunic first, then at the tufts of hair on his knees. Bill moaned in pain and pleasure when the hair ripped out at the roots and returned the favor as Fester's knees became available.

Then they were face to face again, a full spin of the bottle. Like greased pigs, they couldn't quite keep hold of each other's bodies, but their teeth repeatedly ripped at hair tufts, sucking it into their mouths at first, then giving it mighty tugs. They grabbed harshly at each other's genitals. Their victory roars filled the room.

"Yuuuuummmm!" screamed the Rankodor.

"Diiiiiiiiiiieeee!" screamed Bill.

Nothing else in the universe mattered. They guffawed and wept, slammed and spanked each other in their soup of sweat until finally both opened their mouths and put their jaws into lock mode. They froze there on the floor, staring at each other, until simultaneously their lunches or dinners, whatever meal that just was, came up on reverse vacuum and spewed over the other.

Orange, yellow, brown, and green gobs that had been barely discernable before eating sprayed on the walls and the tunics, but they weren't done. Not wanting to waste good food, they slurped up each other's partially digested glop until the chunks were gone and nothing remained but slimy, stained puddles.

Now they were done. They were spent, and both knew it, at exactly the same time. It was over.

Exhausted, Bill closed his eyes and fell immediately into a deep sleep. In the distance, he heard the thunderous snores of Fester, but it was like white noise to his ears.

Chapter 27: Working at the Car Wash

When he woke, Bill stood and could barely wrestle his foot from the floor, it being so stuck to the ground in the goop that had come from both Rankodors. It had started to congeal and harden, and Bill gagged a little before thinking to close his eyes. He held BG over the nostrils of his muzzle.

He left Fester still in the throes of some nightmare, twitching and sending little balls of gunk onto the walls of the room.

"Um. Thank you?" he whispered as he grabbed his schtick and exited. He looked both ways in the hallway, then decided to follow a blinking yellow light that read 'SWISHERUPPER.'

"This makes significant sense," he muttered under his breath, which tasted sour and milky. He clamped his muzzle shut and followed the signs. Sure enough, Rankodors in all stages of goopiness were waiting their turns at the entry to what sounded like the mechanical swishing of an old Earth car wash.

Bill watched carefully as the Rankodor in front of him calmly stepped through a door, guided by another Rankodor who motioned with his hands to continue to come forward. Then the hands did a stop sign, and the Rankodor started to glide forward on a conveyor belt.

When it was his turn, Bill nodded politely at the guide and followed signed instructions to take his tunic off. Without a thought, Bill stripped and handed the guide the garment, and watched as it was sent into a wringer that spouted bubbles amid the smell of musty carpet. Then Bill started moving through a system of swishing brushes that slapped at his body with soap that smelled of wet dog and hot sudsy water.

Slow but sure, all the stickiness and oily secretions were washed away. Another guide beside the conveyor belt wore a wet suit and showed Bill how to stand in the next phase, legs apart and hands extended, looking at the ceiling. Bill complied.

Hot steamy water sloshed over his face, washed away the bubbles on his body and was followed by freezing cold sprays that buffeted him from all sides. He sputtered but wasn't put off in the slightest. It was as if he'd been doing this all his life and loving it.

But he hadn't, he realized with a start. He needed to concentrate, before the Rankodor in him became famished or lusty or thirsty or sleepy or horny, again. He needed to move. Toward Kimra, toward the *Tenuous Hope*, which really was his only salvation, as far as he could see it.

"Caution. The moving walkway is coming to an end," said an automated female voice above him. For just a moment, Bill Griffin lost himself in her sultry come-on, but then the wash was over, another guide presented Bill's tunic to him, completely de-slimed, and then the Rankodor did a little weird curtsy as he reverently lifted Bill's schtick up for BG to accept.

Bill gave a proper nod and wondered if this Rankodor could be his sparring partner Fester of Whatever and Whoever. They all looked alike. He shrugged and moved toward where he thought the prison was, through the massive tavern-like room where he had eaten. He ignored the rumble in his stomach.

Life was not going to continue this way, he knew. He felt just a glimmer of a shift in his thought processes and knew. The crazy insatiable Ralf was soon to turn into good old reliable Bill Griffin, and he needed to get the fuck out of Rankor before that happened and all hell broke loose.

Exiting the main hall, he wound his way through the tunnels until he arrived back at the holding cells.

"There he is," said a guard outside of Kimra's cell. "This is the guy." He reached out with his schtick and gave Bill a good poke in the stomach. "You. Blue Balzar the Great has arrived and will grace us soon to inspect the prisoners."

"Wha?" Bill looked behind him as if thinking maybe the guard was talking to someone else. "Okay, great? Um. That means I will be collecting my reward?" He gave a mean chuckle and the guard sneered in conspiracy.

"She is a nasty one, eh?" commented the guard. He put his schtick up in the air and Bill brought his up to meet it, mimicking a fencing pose, but instead of a combative strike, the schticks made contact as if to caress each other.

"Like a robot, right?" Bill gave a guffaw but caught the angry look of Kimra behind the guard, and his smile disappeared.

"*Like* a robot. HA! She *is* a robot!" The guard sidled up to Bill, dangerously close, so close Bill could smell its gamey breath. Bill inhaled and closed his eyes. He was just starting to lean in with his schtick when Kimra's voice came to him, loud and clear.

Chapter 28: Yertle Blues

What on Rankor have you been up to? We could have been killed or taken away while you were out cavorting. Explain yourself, Bill Griffin.

Bill looked at the guard to see if Kimra's words were indeed inside his head or if she was actually speaking aloud. The guard sashayed back and forth in front of Kimra's cell, stroking and admiring his schtick. Bill forced himself to look away.

Apologies, Kimra. I've been fighting. Or fucking. Or maybe both. I'm sorry. It's just my Rankodor nature, I'm afraid.

Well, fight your damned shifting nature, Griffin! We have to stick to the plan. Now concentrate! We need you for this! Kimra's telepathic thoughts were harsh and unforgiving.

Um. About the plan, Kimra? Bill looked at her beseechingly. *With all good intentions, you have no idea how difficult, or actually how easy, it is. Being a Rankodor, I mean. I have no way of holding on to an idea for any longer than my critical organs will allow.*

Critical organs? Kimra shot Bill a questioning look, her brows furrowed.

Yes. What matters to these creatures, to us, is our stomachs and our sex organs. And then sleep. It's marvelous, in a way. But if you could just review the plan with me, I'm sure I'll catch up. I think. Bill's telepathic thoughts betrayed the worry he felt as he caught just a glimpse of his knee hair disappearing. *I think we need to hurry a bit. I might be shifting back.*

What fresh hell is this? Kimra's eyes widened in alarm. *All we need of you, Bill, is to clear a path for us. From here to the* Last Vestige. *If there are any guards between here and there, you need to get them out of our way. Distract them. Incapacitate them however you can. Use BG. Concentrate and let BG lead the way. We have our own plan on the actual escape from the cells.*

Bill looked at the guard, who was distracted, trying to pick at something deep in its nostril. Before Bill could think of his next move, his thoughts were interrupted with Kimra's thoughts again.

Oh, there has been a minor change of plans. Besides Ryval and myself, we now have another to bring along. Yew.

Wait, what? Bill was confused. He scratched his crotch and some hair came off into his hand. *You want to bring me along, but you want me to clear the path for you?*

Not YOU, Bill Griffin. Yew. Kimra gave Bill an exasperated look.

Hmmm. Seems my hearing is playing tricks on me. Bill thought about plates full of lumpy meat stuff and licked his lips. He was getting a little bored here.

Yew, Y-E-W, is the NAME of the other that we need to bring along, Bill Griffin. Don't worry about getting full explanations for it. Just go and clear a path! Blue Balzar is nearby and we must get off of Rankor quickly, before you shift and before he corners us! Please! I'll send you a signal when we're clear to run.

Wait. Bill looked hesitant. *You'll send me a signal? Or you'll send this Yew a signal?*

Gaa, Bill Griffin! You're making me short circuit! Don't worry about the details. Just clear the path and keep in contact with my voice. Kimra dismissed Bill with a brief, but highly effective, snarl on her face.

"Grouch," Bill said aloud. The guard stopped picking his nose and looked up with a question in his eyes.

"Who, me?" he asked.

"Well not Yew, that's for sure," Bill said. "I'll be off on a bit of a break now. Nice links, by the way." He smiled when the guard modestly stole a look at his cufflinks, giant ancient coins with some man's face on them. Bill touched his forehead with what he hoped was casual nonchalance and walked away, toward the threshold where he had originally entered with Kimra.

Okay, now to clear a path. Clear a path. Clear a path. Bill made his way slowly past the cells, noticing again how perfectly sculpted Ryval's features were, with that sharp chiseled chin. He paused in admiration for just a moment before seeing Kimra's threatening glare. He gave a silent salute and marched down the corridor.

Tell me what you see, insisted Kimra.

I see troughs of green? And red noses too. I see their schticks... for poking you. And I stink to myself... what a rankodor w—

Damn it all, Griffin! Just pay attention for a few more minutes, will you?

Oopsies, Kimra sounded angry again. Still. Obviously, she was not a Louis Armstrong fan, if she even knew of the Earth legend.

Bill's eyes had teared up, singing that song that sort of reminded him of home. The sadness made him snap out of his Rankodor thoughts. Concentrate, you big-assed baby. BG.

Home, thought Bill, feeling the sting of tears again. He sped up his pace despite the momentary sadness. So far, the corridor had been empty, almost echoing his footsteps as he shuffled forward. But then he stopped and stood still, like a rabbit caught in a hawk's sight. Before him stood the tallest living creature he had ever seen.

Taller than Rikki, maybe standing ten feet high, the thing stood with its profile to Bill. Its torso was encased in a shell that looked like rippling leather, and from what Bill could tell, the shell was part of this guy's actual body, not just a shield.

The giant carried a long schtick, but like no other schtick Bill had ever seen on Rankor or anywhere else. It was like a Halberd-Mace spear, with a dramatically oversized hatchet head at its peak, and it shone like titanium under the lights of the hall.

Bill licked his lips and noticed with alarm that his muzzle was starting to shrink.

"Excuse me? Sir?" He gave an apologetic smile to the giant while trying not to gasp at the sight of the guy's face up close. Like a true snapper in old Aunt Em's back pond, the creature had a horny layered protuberance that overlapped its mouth, and on top of that beak-ish nose were four tiny eyes, now narrowed and focused on Bill Griffin.

Bill reached up with his schtick to greet the gargantuan turtle man. He poked at the shell in a fraternal kind of way and smiled again, but the beast slammed his spear against Bill's chest and pressed him against the wall. The four eyes were right in front of Bill's slowly dissolving muzzle, and the breath coming out of that beaky mouth smelled of swamp and decay.

Bill coughed politely, and the thing pulled back as if to gag. Bill remembered that not everyone thought he smelled as lovely as he thought he did.

"Sorry to surprise you," he said, trying to speak from the side of his mouth so as not to offend.

"Be gone, Smell Bucket," the turtle man said.

"But I—"

"I said *be gone!* Master Blue Balzar's ship approaches as we speak. You will do nothing but offend his sensibilities."

"I'll do my very best to stay out of his way, but you need to understand how things work here, sir. I am here as a welcoming agent of my planet Rankor. It's my duty." Bill looked around him nervously, wondering how the hell he could possibly distract or incapacitate this beast. "Sorry, did you give me your name?" He stuck his schtick out for good will.

"I am Wangba. And no, your presence will do anything *but* welcome Master," said the turtle man. "You smell like an old sponge from a toilet."

"Wha?" Bill felt fury build in him but tamped it down. *Remember Kimra. Remember the plan. What was the plan? Remember home. Clarity.*

"Never mind your smell. Master has placed me here in advance of his landing. He is working on heightened security. Lucky for your smelly self, Master is in a good mood. He had not counted on the robot woman as well as golden hair." Wangba stuck out his tongue that looked like a triangular rock and touched it to his beak.

"Say," Bill said with what he hoped was a buddy kind of tone. "You look famished. And wait until you get a load of our cocktail list. While we wait for the illustrious Blue Balzar's ship and your reinforcements, how about I pay your tab at the bar? The service is quick, and you look a little dehydrated, my friend."

Bill's neck was starting to ache from staring straight up into all four of those creepy eyes. He reached into his tunic pocket and took out the packet of photos Kimra had given him eons ago, the pictures from Earth. He unfolded them. The one he placed in Wangba's hands was the cover from a women's magazine that flashed a half-dressed beauty of a human with ruby red lips and hair to match. She wore a gauzy gown that was open in the front. The dress just barely covered an incredible set of erect nipples, and her white creamy breasts bulged to get out.

With a jolt of excitement, Bill realized that this Wangba dude was biting at the easy bait. The four eyes blinked in unison as the creature pondered his options.

"Really," Bill said. "It's on me. This should more than cover dinner and drinks."

"Fine. Sold. Master Blue is expected, but not for another quarter blitz. I will relieve myself and renew my liquids and be back long before then." The corded muscles in Wangba's neck strained and stretched and his eyes bugged out like four fat legs on an ottoman.

Bill watched as the turtle man ambled down the corridor, swishing his spear-schtick back and forth between hands.

Bill closed his eyes and tried his hardest to concentrate. He rested his hand on BG and felt it pulse.

Kimra? Kimra, you there?

I heard the whole thing, Bill Griffin. Well done. Meet us back at the cell and be prepared to improvise, please.

Chapter 29: Gotta Get Outta This Place

Nothing seemed out of the ordinary as Bill approached the prison area. He opened the main gate to the corridor where the cells lined up, and he could see Ryval's fashionable boots thrust out from the corner shadows. Kimra remained huddled in an opposite corner of the cell next to Ryval's. Her metallic skin and dress reflected the dim light around her.

No sign of Yew. Bill sent his thought out to no one in particular. No one answered. Maybe they were all asleep? But how could that be, when he had just heard from them and everyone seemed ready to bust out?

Everything okay? he asked very pointedly. Nothing in return.

A hint of panic began chewing at Bill's innards when Kimra's thoughts finally cut in. He thought, though, that he heard the word *Stall.* He exited the cell corridor and once again joined the Rankodor guard with the coin cuffs.

"Can't *wait* for the Balzar *Master*!" Bill said, clapping his hands like a child, getting into the act. His voice was a little squeaky and he felt sweaty, oily all of a sudden. He heard just the slightest shuffle behind the entranceway to the cells and kept squeaking. "Get my *rewards!* Yeah, *Baby!* Fill up the pockets, Buddy! Come on! Argh!" He curled his arms into a bodybuilder pose and widened his eyes. "Am I *right*? Is it bonus time, or *WHAT*?" He wagged his little nub of a tail and chortled.

Bill noticed one of the guards cock his head as Bill waddled up to the door leading to the cell station. The Rankodor guard gave a snort and waved his hand for Bill to stop talking.

"Payday, *today*, brothers or sisters, *hey* now!" Bill clapped again as another guard joined the first at the entranceway. Together, they looked like a couple of dogs listening for their master's car in the garage. Bill swallowed and kept going.

"Blue Balzar forever, I say!"

Finally, CoinCuff guard approached him and gave Bill a firm poke in the ribs with his schtick. "Silence, MouthMan!" Another poke in the shoulder and CoinCuff joined the other two Rankodors at the cell station's main gate. Behind it, there was a clank, like a lid getting slammed onto a pot, then silence.

Bill cleared his throat and opened his mouth, but CoinCuff made a grimace that stopped him cold. All four Rankodors froze, though, when they heard a soft but definitive shave-and-a-haircut knock on the opposite side of the entranceway.

"Who in the name of Great God Rancid could be in there? Other than the prisoners, I mean?" asked CoinCuff. He pulled at a wad of hair on his eyelid then bit his lip. "Identify yourself!" he shouted at the gate. To the other guards, he whispered, "It is not possible that they could have gotten out of the cells. Who fed them last?" He glared at each Rankodor in turn.

A voice, confident and strong, came from the other side of the gate. "No, it is I, GreatGuano! All is well. I just fell asleep in here, that's all. Blue Balzar has indeed requested the prisoners be taken to his ship which is landing any moment now, though! Bounties and bonuses will be paid upon delivery! Open up!"

"Wha?" CoinCuff Rankodor lifted his lips and narrowed his eyes. "Who is GreatGuano? There is no Rankodor with that name on the roster. Don't—"

But it was too late. One of the other dullards had already opened the cell corridor's main gate in his frenzy for bonus magazine clippings. Bill felt BG come alive and he gave an excited grin which probably came across as a goofy sneer to the other Rankodors.

The gate swung open. Kimra was the first thing Bill saw, shining and perfect. She assessed the situation in the room, her eyes and skin circuitry flashing and confusing the Rankodor guards. As she stepped forward, Bill felt more than saw the presence of Ryval. Ryval captured the attention of everyone in the room, stunning the guards for just an instant as if he had hypnotic control.

And in that instant, Bill saw her. It had to be Yew. Standing at a diminutive four feet, maybe a tad more, her perfectly proportioned body was wrapped in a pale yellow and pink gauze that was completely see-through except for one tiny patch between her legs. Her hair was golden and tied up at the very top of her head, cascading down in a shining ponytail that bounced, as did her breasts, where Bill's eyes finally rested.

That one stunned moment was time well spent. All three prisoners were in flight mode, and Bill rose to the occasion.

BG led the way. Bill reached for the first guard and ran his third finger up the crack of the guard's ass.

"Touch," Bill whispered. He dipped his other hand's index finger into the second guard's ear. "Mmmm," he moaned.

The guards had turned to stone, it seemed. Their eyes glazed over, their mouths hung open, and Bill gave them the cherry on top with a lick on each of their eyelids. With gentle nudges of his schtick, Bill pushed the guards over.

Kimra followed his lead. She had taken CoinCuffs by the wrists and massaged them, whispering in a flinty, breathy voice. CoinCuffs didn't respond quite as dramatically as the other two had, so Bill hurried to Kimra's side.

"I think they need a real rank odor, so to speak," Bill said with a smile. He opened his mouth and exhaled onto CoinCuff's muzzle and BG lit up to help. Bill placed BG just behind the Rankodor's knee, squeezed gently, and was aptly rewarded with that oily, creamy goo he'd washed off his body nearly a half-blitz ago.

The reminder of his recent Rankodor behavior hit him with a grip of dread. BG started to resemble the old BG that had been attached to his human self. He touched his own face and felt a strange mixture of relief and fear when he found no random tufts of hair. He looked over his shoulder in the direction of the bar and saw that other Rankodors had noticed the commotion he was causing. Some headed their way.

"Touch," he said, in an unintentionally loud voice, and he pushed good old CoinCuffs over. All three guards remained stunned in frozen lumps by the inappropriate touching, their schticks pointed up at the ceiling from their piles of goo.

"Follow me!" Bill yelled. Kimra, Ryval, and Yew took off toward the exit tunnel behind Bill. The oncoming Rankodors gave chase.

"Haul ass, gang!" shouted Bill, as he stopped at the tunnel to let his friends through.

"I'm still unsure as to the reason why I was unable to stun them as you were," Kimra said as she passed Bill.

"Pedal to the metal, Kimra," Bill said. "Actually, maybe it was the metal or in this case, flesh. Maybe Rankodors need a touch of actual flesh to get them going." He looked over his shoulder and nodded to the other two. "Touch them right behind the knees. Squeeze like it's a giant zit. Then go for the eyelid. Tongue works, too, but might prove difficult."

"Anus. Don't forget the anus," added Ryval.

Bill looked up at the sound of the first words that he would hear from those silky lips, the new voice that was almost a croon, most certainly sexy, considering the words referred to Rankodor asshole. Bill smiled back at Ryval and hoisted his schtick in agreement.

"Also, the umbilical nerve pinch," Kimra said, as a couple of Rankodors caught up with them. She reached under the tunic of the closest one and tweaked the smelly creature's belly button, or at least Bill thought it was a belly button. The Rankodor stopped with a jolt, clamped its muzzle shut while a glaze came over its eyes. She pushed it over.

"Metal seems to have performed fine on that one," she said.

Yew hadn't said a word yet, but being so slight, she was able to run with grace and speed. When one of the pursuers caught up with her, she turned to get behind it and dug her fingers into its knee. The Rankodor turned a distinct gray. Yew's exclamation of surprise, Bill thought, sounded like angels singing.

The Rankodor that turned gray fell backward into the stream of oncoming Rankodors, until at last the whole debacle turned into a giant dominos effect. As they fell onto and touched each other with more than just their simple schticks, Bill heard a chant grow.

"Get a Room! Get a Room!" Louder and louder it came, echoing through the exit tunnel. The reverie of distraction built until all the Rankodors joined forces and retreated to their sacred fuck or fight rooms.

"Okay, gang," Bill huffed between ragged breaths, "let's get our bearings for a second. We'll hunker down and get a feel for timing, here. Try to be inconspicuous in case we get any stragglers."

He looked first to Kimra, gleaming and strangely sexy, then to Ryval, the perfect god-like, male specimen. Then Bill looked at the exposed and exciting Yew. "Okay, well, so much for inconspicuous, I guess."

Bill studied the exit ramp, then looked back toward the tunnel, and at the far end of it stood turtle guy, Wangba. He had stretched his neck forward to see better, and he was lumbering into the tunnel.

"Um," said Bill. "Let's hope that this guy lives up to the turtle's reputation. I don't think we can stay hidden anymore. Now it's just a race." He pulled at a tuft on his shoulder. "A race between tortoise and hair. Let's *go!*"

Chapter 30: Please Act Normal

Bill led the way toward the docking bay entrance, with Ryval right on his heels, and Kimra not far behind. Yew trailed along in the rear, but Bill got the feeling it was on purpose. She continually crisscrossed behind them as if to ward off any oncoming enemies, her shiny ponytail and breasts bobbing as she ran.

Behind them, Wangba made up for lost time, and Bill could hear the Rankodors panicking as the turtle man tossed them aside to clear his path.

Talk about unearthly sounds! Bill thought.

He smiled sadly at the reference, pondering what it really meant anymore. Everything was unearthly now, wasn't it? Life had certainly been interesting in the recent past, more interesting than your average moon janitor's existence. Still, Bill knew in his heart that there would always be a void where home should be.

Somewhere up ahead was a ship that carried the man who had destroyed his home. He looked behind him. That Blue Balzar dude had also taken the homes of everyone here, not just him. And now that scrawny moon maintenance man was leading the way, escaping a crazy cartoon planet and the Blue man, only to plot a way to destroy that man and any who served him.

Bill Griffin would find a way.

He stopped abruptly as they got within sight of the docking bay, a prodigious array berthing several ships from other star systems. At the vestibule, a single sleeping Rankodor snored and spit out little gobs of goo. He wore cuffs with links of glass eyeballs. Bill reached down and caressed its stomach, and it woke with a jolt.

"What the—"

"Shhh, little one," Bill said, as if to a child. "Shhhh."

He ran his hands behind the Rankodor's knee and gave it a good solid but sexy squeeze. The Rankodor's eyes bulged out, and that milky sweat oozed out from his pores. And then it slept a deeper sleep.

As he watched the creature sleep, Bill looked down at BG, now almost at its original configuration, blinking wild colors and flashing signals Bill still didn't know how to translate.

"Well," said Kimra as she joined him, "you're certainly becoming less odious, Bill Griffin."

"Wow, thanks, Kimra. You always know what to say to make a guy feel special." He patted her on her back and smiled at the clanking sound it made. "While we're on the subject, though, wasn't this Rankodor form supposed to last a full blitz? Seems like it hasn't been three hours. Maybe time flies while you're having fun?"

"Hmm," she said, looking him square in the eyes until he started to feel uncomfortable. "Sometimes a shifting phase moves faster if the organism in question has been expending energy in overly strenuous ways.

Might you have taxed your physical being to the point of total exhaustion?"

Bill stared at her.

"Well, no matter," he answered, looking back over her shoulder to see Wangba heading their way. "Glad I'm not odiferous. Or whatever you just said. We have to get the blue blazes outta here, Kimra."

"Yes. But see that?" She pointed to an enormous rocket-shaped ship. It was brilliant sky blue, with navy blue details depicting birds in flight on its sides, and a white crescent moon just below an image of a bridge.

"Yeah," Bill said. "Balzar's?"

"Balzar's, indeed." Kimra nodded her head as Ryval and Yew joined them.

"What in the Milky Way are those things outside it?" Ryval asked.

Standing just outside the blue ship were two stick-thin creatures with many skinny appendages, almost praying mantis like, Bill thought. Their legs moved as if on their own accord, with knees or elbows bending at unnatural angles, and their green heads swiveled in all directions.

"I'm thinking if we just act normal, cool, and nonchalant, we can make it to the *Vestige*. Keep our heads and this should work." He started whistling and sauntering across the tarmac toward the *Last Vestige*, which was looking shiny and welcoming. Not home, but as close as he could get to it.

The others started to follow. "Normal?" Ryval asked. "Just what is normal about making strange trilling sounds between one's lips and strolling as if test-driving a new schtick?"

"Get down!" Bill said as BG lit up with a red alarm. All four hit the pavement. Just as Bill wished the merry band had more cover, BG emitted a cloud of vapor that surrounded them with cool, foggy protection.

"Well, now. How 'bout them apples," Bill said. "Apparently BG has detected that the grasshopper mantis guys have spotted us, and that our slow-moving Wangba friend is speeding up somehow. Screw nonchalant and normal, let's run if everyone can handle that?" Bill looked at Yew because she was the smallest.

"Wait. Sir?" Yew piped up. Bill looked her way, at her breasts, and she rolled her eyes. "Eyes are up here? Are we still going for normal?"

"Forget normal, Yew!" Ryval shouted, as he started running for the *Last Vestige*, with Bill following his lead. Even on one Rankodor leg and one human, even at an awkward, hip jolting waddle, Bill managed to get past Ryval.

A familiar little chirp came to him through the cloud, and suddenly there was Qeet, perched on his shoulder, his eyeballs googling into Bill's.

"Step on it, Maggot! Double time it to the ship! Last maggot on board gets TP duty for a hundred blitzes! Or a week! Whatever a week is! Hut! Hut! Hut!" Qeet chanted jubilantly, waving his bird arms in the air as Bill loped on his still shifting leg.

"Qeet! Good to see you, my fluffy bird-monkey-brained friend," Bill said between breaths. "I'm going as fast as I can. And have you been watching old Earth vids to expand that vocab of yours?"

"Yes, Bill Maggot Griffin. I have been studying military history. You remind me of that great warrior, Gomer."

They felt it then, a scraping and scratching on the pavement beneath their feet, and Bill knew those insect guards were on their heels, even if they couldn't see them. The good guys reached the ship, and Kimra deftly took to the manual controls, releasing the docking clamps.

As they ran up the ramp to enter the *Last Vestige*, Kimra said, "I have already overridden the planet security protocols. The navigational and systems boards are powering up as we speak. Secure yourselves."

The hatch had barely slid to an air-tight seal when Bill saw the giant turtle beast through the starboard porthole beside the helm. Wangba squashed his face against the window, his stony tongue clicking at the polymer-silicon glass. Bill pulled away from the porthole in alarm as the creature hacked at the ship with his menacing spear schtick.

"This might be a good time to take off!" Bill shouted.

"As you wish. You don't have to yell," said Kimra as Bill felt the shuttle move.

Feeling less shaken, he looked at his dim reflection in the porthole, watching the receding grasshopper guards and giant turtle disappear into the distance.

From what he could see of himself in the semi-reflective window, all was human once again. Maybe the hair still had a ways to go, he mused, combing BG's fingers through it. Everything else from Ralf had disappeared.

Except the schtick. He still had his schtick.

Chapter 31: Blue By Yew

"Well, whew, that's about all I can say," Bill said as they watched Rankor slowly shrink away in the infinity of space. Kimra kept her focus on the helm, checking the controls and maneuvering the shuttle toward the *Tenuous Hope.* Bill breathed easier, swallowed easier now that he had completely lost the Rankodor mucous strands that had run down his throat.

"Bill Griffin. Please introduce yourself properly to our guests, now that the danger has passed," said Kimra, her attention still on the shuttle's controls.

"Ah," said Bill, thrusting his right hand out toward Ryval and looking him directly in the eyes, just like Aunt Em had taught him so long ago. "Bill Griffin. Happy to make your acquaintance. Happy to help. Happy to rescue. Uh." He gave a little apologetic smile.

"Ryval Marzz." He grabbed Bill's hand in a firm grip and shook vigorously. "Appreciate what you did for us back there. Well done."

"Oh, the *Tenuous Hope* crew went out of their way for me, first, actually, which is why Captain Rane is a bit put out with me. You were her main mission and objective. I'm just the boulder in the middle of their stream, I'm afraid," said Bill.

"I am not understanding?" interjected Yew, searching both men's eyes for clarification. "You are a rock man? You are made of stones?"

"Bill," said Ryval, "meet Yew. One thing you'll need to know about Yew is that she takes everything, and I mean everything, literally. Therefore, clichés, turns of phrases, or puns might get you into hot water, if you know what I mean."

"This water," said Yew, "is the stream where rock man comes from? Yes?"

"I'm sorry," said Bill, with his hand extended to shake hers, "No, Yew. I'm not made of stones, and there is no water. I just meant that I've been a bit of an inconvenience to the captain and crew of the *Tenuous Hope*. Apologies for the misunderstanding." He smiled easily at Ryval. "Thanks for the tip."

"Anytime," Ryval said, staring at BG with its smooth buttonless tricked out display of intermittent flashing lights.

"So!" said Bill, "Rankor was crazy, right? So, so hard to keep my wits about me while I was in the form of a Rankodor, I tell ya. The *slop* they eat, wow, as a human that must've been *horrendous* for you, right?"

"Who said anything about my being a human, Bill?" Ryval gave a little tug to his shirt cuffs to straighten them.

"Oh. Sorry. I guess I was just excited to see another person. You look like a person, you see. I mean a human person. Man. Which was also exciting to me. To see another man. Not," Bill put his hands up, "Not that I'm *excited*, excited to see a man, you understand. I like women. Love women, actually. But you know, I thought I'd never see another man. Ever again." He finally petered out, lost in the effort of conversation.

But then as he realized that Yew and Ryval seemed perfectly comfortable not talking at all, he still pressed on, picking at any conversational thread he could muster. "Did you know," he said, his eyes brightening up, "that Rankodors pull out tufts of each other's hair during... uh, during the sex act? At least that's what I overheard. In the bar. Crazy, right?"

"I had heard that, yes," said Ryval with a polite smile. Yew hid her laugh behind her tiny hands like a little girl with a secret. "But how did you lose yours, then?" Ryval pointed up at Bill's head to a couple of places and Bill blanched.

"Um..."

To his relief, Bill was interrupted by Qeet's happy little chirrup. Qeet had teleported onto Yew's shoulder and had turned a brilliant golden blond. He brushed up against Yew's ponytail and buried his head in her tresses to breathe her in. The fuss made Ryval turn his head away from Bill, revealing several naked spots on the back of his head. Bill's eyes widened, and he suppressed a snort.

"Oh," Bill started again, "I guess what happens in prison stays in prison, right? I mean, everyone tells you bad things happen to you there. That's half the motivation they give you for not shoplifting, am I right?" He gave a loud guffaw and slapped BG onto his knee.

"Qeet know who Yew are," said Qeet, after taking several more whiffs of Yew's hair.

"It is actually who Yew *is*, not who Yew are," said Ryval, "but we know what you are trying to say."

Qeet looked at him for a second then went on. "Yew very powerful. Yew magic. Bill Griffin call Yew genie. Or leprechaun? Or faery? Not sure. Yew grant wishes."

"Ah," said Bill. "Well, isn't that something. How do you know Yew, Qeet?"

"Famous story, Bill Griffin. Yew reason Blue Balzar be blue!"

"What?" Ryval exclaimed. "I was told that Yew is the reason for Blue Balzar's power. Not his color."

"No, Ryval Marzz," said Qeet.

"Blue Balzar is the worst kind of monster, an untrustworthy creature," said Yew, her eyes dark with memory. "When he released me from my prison, he was a hero to me. Well, you can imagine, being trapped in a nutshell for millions of blitzes. I granted him a wish, was happy to do so, mind you."

"Wait, you were actually in a nutshell?" Bill asked.

"Indeed. Until that day when Blue Balzar chipped his tooth on it and I was magically released. I was very grateful, so I granted him a wish."

"And what did he wish for, Yew?" Ryval asked.

"Turns out, in the long run, yes." Yew's eyes watered for a moment and she blinked.

"No, I mean, what did he wish for?"

"Oh, his wish had a story of its own," said Yew. "He told me of his birthday of twenty-one, whatever that might mean. He told me his fraternity brothers, which by the way is a redundancy in itself, now that I have had time to study that conversation. Anyway, his brothers bought him a woman. Imagine that, buying a woman! And this woman, Blue Balzar told me, asked him what he wanted, just as I was asking him what he wanted. And then he told me. The woman blue him. He said it was incredible. He said it felt like heaven." Yew made air quotes when she said 'heaven' in a resentful, snippy way.

There was an awkward moment as they all, even Qeet, looked down at the floor. Kimra cleared her throat but didn't turn away from the helm.

"And…" Ryval started. "You turned him blue."

"Exactly. Just as he requested. I blue him."

"Ah," Bill said. "Something got lost in translation. And he got angry?"

"He did!" Yew's eyes widened and she stood up. "I had given him what he wished, but somehow that was not the way he had wanted it? And he reached for me, but I poofed out. Ever since that day, he has made my existence a misery, following me everywhere, no matter where in the galaxy I tread. He shouts evil, vile things at me every time he catches up to me. Tells me that one day he will imprison me in his nut sack. I find him dishonorable and quite unreasonable."

Kimra turned at that point and raised her eyebrows. "Is this 'nut sack' Yew describes something that is traditionally used as a threat or prison on Earth, Bill

Griffin? Is the act of slicing open one's 'nut sack' a 'normal' line of revenge or punishment?"

"On Earth? Well, a guy's nuts are like his treasures. We call them balls, too. They're a guy's most sensitive spot. Where he could physically get a kind of pleasure or pain that he couldn't possibly get anywhere else. And human men are super conscious of any threat to our nuts, like when you were injecting me down there, remember, Kimra? So, no, this guy doesn't sound like he's playing with a full deck, threatening to slice his own nut sack open to cram Yew inside, right?"

Bill hung his head in embarrassment, but then a thought occurred to him. "Wait, what does that have to do with Blue Balzar, though? He's not from Earth…"

But then he stopped, furrowed his brow, and remembered back in the K-torium, when he had done his original research on Balzar, and how weird it was that the data listed Mosington, Virginia as Balzar's hometown, when Mosington was really Bill Griffin's hometown.

He shook his head to clear it. Maybe some bits of Rankodor were still in there, rattling his brains around.

Chapter 32: Crush

"Let me bring some clarity to the issue, here," said Ryval, as he watched Bill's eyes glaze over. "We believe that yes, there is a strong possibility that Blue Balzar actually did come from your small blue planet. I am not familiar with the names of cities or towns on Earth, though. Therefore, I can not help you there. Mosington, Virginia certainly rings a bell, but that could be just from speculative research."

"Well, I did not blue him on the blue planet. I'm sure of that. I know exactly where I was not when that happened," said Yew.

Bill concentrated on Yew's perky breasts. This conversation was starting to hurt his head and the distraction was welcome.

"Here, Bill Griffin," said Kimra, suddenly at his side and away from the helm. She held out a bottle of a liquid that bubbled. He smiled up at her in gratitude. She was a good listener.

"Anyway." Ryval waved away Yew and Bill and the whole Earth conversation. "What truly matters, as far as fallout and outcome are concerned, is what we have learned about Blue Balzar's current state of affairs, and his association with the Jyrx." He looked at Bill's questioning, yet amused eyes and rolled his own.

"Jyrx is the growing band of evil that has infiltrated and enslaved both intelligent and not-so-intelligent beings to use in building class-based societies throughout the galaxy. "

Bill looked at him and took a swallow of the bubbly stuff. "You talk like Kimra. Anyone ever tell you that you talk like Kimra?"

"I am quite sure you mean that as a compliment, Bill, but good one!" And here Ryval threw his head back for a big belly laugh. "Kimra has no sense of humor, but will laugh at the strangest things, which I find downright odd. And you will find that to be a critical difference between us. Humor is paramount in our day and age, do you not agree, to have the ability to laugh and make merry?" He touched his nose and sniffed.

"Okay. Sure." Bill wasn't sure what Ryval's point was, but he could play along.

"Anyway," Ryval went on, "what matters here for the time being is how we proceed. We know that finding and rescuing our Lorde is of primary importance if other goals are to be achieved."

Bill couldn't help himself. "Our Lord? Who's our Lord, again?"

"Lorde Velt herself. The apple of all our eyes. A creature of unparalleled beauty, intelligence, bravery, and wisdom. The summation of all things wise and wonderful. Our leader, our queen, our one and only Lorde Velt. She has been imprisoned by the Jyrx, and my recently acquired intel points us to the planet of

Sqinitree in the Sextons B system, just over one million parsecs from here, actually."

"That's crazy, man," said Bill.

"Ah, fear not when it comes to traveling through space, Bill. We have all kinds of tech to make that kind of jump."

"No, not the distance," said Bill. "The name. Lord Velt."

"Is it because it sounds like someone you know from Earth?" asked Kimra from her workstation.

"Maybe, I'm not sure. Lord Velt. Lord Velt." He tapped BG to his forehead. "It's been bugging me since I first heard it. And now I remember a similar name, Lord Roosevelt was this gaming dude on Earth. We were on the same team."

"You ate bugs while hunting for small beasts to eat with *Lorde Roosevelt*?" asked Yew.

"No, no, sorry, Yew. I played vid games with a kid on Earth who had a moniker, a name, I mean, just for gaming. He called himself Lord Roosevelt. Virtually, I mean. I never met him. But he kicked ass, let me tell you. It's just crazy, that's all. That the names could be so similar. The world is getting smaller the more I learn." He hummed softly, clapping BG against his other hand that held his bubbly. He gave a feeble smile as the others looked at him in silence.

"Ah," said Ryval, clearly disinterested in Bill Griffin's Earth games. "Well, this Lorde Velt is most definitely a female. The most beautiful of all females, I must say. She is quite unmatched in all the combined worlds, in the entire universe. She is my tether to pure peace and happiness. When I am in her presence, time stands perfectly still, and I am there. Now." His eyes closed, and his nostrils flared as he took deep, rich breaths.

"Okay," Bill said, taking another drink. "Sounds like an intense crush on your part, Ryval."

"Crush? I know not the meaning of your word 'crush,' Bill Griffin, but let me tell you and redefine for you how it is with me. What I have, on my part, as you say, is intense adoration and a deep, abiding love for this goddess of all space. Which sounds just a bit larger and more important than your word 'crush.' Just because we have not had a chance to profess our mutual love does not indicate a lack of said love." Ryval gave another sniff, this time with a definite sound of indignation.

Bill patted Qeet's little head as he listened and gave Ryval a sad smile. "Apologies, Ryval. I didn't mean to make light of how you feel toward your goddess. I think I know what that kind of love feels like. Had one of my own back on Earth. But I never spoke of it. Never approached her. Never had the balls to tell her the truth." He felt a lump in his gullet that he tried to drink away. He cleared his throat.

"And now? She's probably dead, just like everyone else I ever knew or loved. And I'm beating myself up for never having said to her, 'Hey, you know what? I think you're the most perfect woman I've ever met in all my life.' I mean, how hard would that have been? To just take the damn purple pen back to her and hand it to her and touch her and smile into her face and maybe lean in—"

"Okay, okay, Bill Griffin, we get the idea," said Yew with a huff.

"Sorry," Bill said. "My point is that life is shorter than we imagine. We should tell the people we love how we feel. Because tonight, any of us could be blown to smithereens."

"Charming," said Kimra, staring into the void of space before them.

"Sorry again. Gosh, I have a lot to be sorry for lately, whew! You'd never know I just rescued a few people from the hands of smelly Rankodors and while I was at it, from the blue man himself, right? Am I right? Well, let me tell you," he said, looking at each of them in turn, "I get to talk sometimes, too. After losing my home and my planet and all of my relatives, at least I'm adapting to the situation at hand."

"You do have a situation at hand, indeed, Bill," said Yew, her eyes dancing.

They all looked at BG. Bill's hand was ablaze like Vegas on steroids.

Chapter 33: Remember Me

At long last, the *Vestige* docked safely within the shuttle bay of the *Tenuous Hope*. Kimra, looking distracted, excused herself, saying she needed to report to Captain Rane immediately, and Bill could have sworn he heard her words whisper something in his head about getting some clarity on this issue. He shook his head again and stuck a BG finger in his ear.

BG's lights were still flashing, but instead of the usual bright primary colors, the tones were soft pastels.

"Maybe your appendage is just excited to be home?" Ryval asked, watching the prosthetic with interest.

"Yes, I'm afraid I still have a lot to learn," Bill said with a smile. He watched Qeet bouncing happily on Yew's shoulder as they made their way down the ramp. Bill turned to Ryval and said in a conspiratorial voice, "Someone has a little crush, I fear."

The two laughed as Qeet buried his face in Yew's hair. Bill started to feel the warm relaxation of safety and some semblance of friendship.

"I do not envy her, that is for certain," Ryval said. "The last time I saw a Qeet with a crush, it struck me as an almost stalking type of situation. Would not leave the poor girl alone, teleporting to her side, then away to get a gift of some sort, then teleporting back. They can be such nuisances, really."

"Aw. This Qeet means well. I'm sure it'll pass," Bill said.

"Well, the two of us, Yew and I, need to undergo a complete physical. Please excuse us," said Ryval.

"Wait, what? You just said that you and I had to get a full-body scan together. Right? Oh," Bill stopped and threw his head back. "This is going to be a challenge, this Yew name. So, you two, Yew and you, need to take care of something. So, I'm being excused. Got it." He made the sign of two pistols from the hip and clicked his tongue. Bill may have been a bit buzzed at this point.

"Qeet hungry! Yew hungry? And You?" Qeet turned back from Yew's shoulder to ask the men.

"I am famished for good food, Qeet," said Ryval, "and I have certainly missed Surrep for more reasons than one. But Surreptitious and feasting will have to wait until after Yew and I are done with our exams."

Bill stopped in mid-step and BG took on new lights as a ball of brown plates rolled toward them.

"Nialme!"

The ball unrolled, the plates clacking against each other like the sound of an antiquated computer keyboard, and Nialme stood before him with a smile on her beautiful lips. She wrapped him in her arms, all warm and soft and smelling fresh, and Bill's knees buckled just a little. He pulled back and held her face in his hands.

"Oh, no, Bill Griffin!" Nialme wrinkled up her nose. "The stench is on you, all over you! And what is this goo? She looked at her hands with disgust, then looked at him accusatorily. "What have you been doing down there, anyway?"

"Well, actually, some might say I've been saving the day, my sweet," Bill gave a chivalrous bow. "Don't have a clue what these folks have in mind, but I can assure you I had a real live part in their release. So, while I might smell and feel gross, it's nothing a little hot water can't fix." He smiled while waving off the others as they went their separate ways.

Walking to his quarters, Bill felt like he was on display with crew members peeking out to watch him pass. Some of them reached out with tentacles or antennae to touch him. They made little sighs of awe. Others took a whiff and retreated behind closed doors. Bill couldn't really blame them. He was ripe.

"What's this all about, anyway?" Bill asked Nialme as they finally made it to his cabin.

"They are in wonderment over you, Bill Griffin." She smiled coyly at Rikki, who didn't speak to them but stood stalk still down the corridor, staring at him. She blinked her enormous eyes and tested the air with her tongue.

Nialme grabbed BG. "It is as you say. You had a part in the release of prominent members of our community. But more importantly, everyone now realizes how valuable human males can be. You are able to hold one of Kimra's shifts for longer than any other species. This mission was a test of her skill, but also of your DNA. And your fortitude assimilating another species' DNA. To keep your wits about you even while managing the physical and visceral properties of a Rankodor is unheard of."

She started undressing him. "This new finding makes you crucial to our long- and short-term efforts as well as a formidable weapon against our enemies."

Off came that nasty tunic, hopefully once and for all. Nialme balled it up and tossed it into the disposal chute discretely tucked away in the cabin wall. Then, when he was all but naked, she gently tugged the cuffs and little Earth links off. She started to throw them down the chute, too, but Bill stopped her.

"No. Please. I want to keep those. Those and the schtick." Nialme placed the links onto the palm of BG, which came alive with light and color.

"You will probably never need them again, Bill Griffin. Well, with any luck, that is!" Nialme chuckled under her breath, but her face became serious when she saw his expression. "What is it? What have I said or done to upset you?"

"Oh, it's not you, Nialme," Bill said, touching her face. "It's just that I have no possessions anymore, you know? My time on that disgusting planet gave me a bit of clarity, though. That life is what you make of it, and sometimes it might actually be good for you to shed your old life and move forward.

"But I'd like to hold on to some things that remind me of that. New memories. New acquaintances, maybe even new friends, however brief our encounters. So," He blinked a couple of times and cleared his throat. "Now I own two Earth cufflinks, a schtick, and one purple pen." He tried to give her a goofy smile but was sure it looked strained.

"Let's shed your old rank odor, now, Bill Griffin," Nialme said softly, and she led him to the running shower that was already filling the room with steam.

She scrubbed his body mercilessly and he let her, closing his eyes and soaking in the suds and hot water. Gone forever the slime of Rankodor, thank God. Between his toes, under his fingernails, down his ass crack, and between his legs, she soaped away the past blitz and a half and all the crud that had accompanied his short yet memorable time there.

Then she re-enacted their previous shower experience, slowly and seductively lapping up the water from every last inch of him, finishing him off in the happiest ending he could have imagined.

"Good?" she asked afterward.

"I think you missed the back of my knees," he said, nodding while he stroked Nialme. Bill may have been inexperienced when it came to women in general and certainly alien females, but BG seemed to have a talent for knowing all the right things to do, all the right places to touch. It didn't take long for Nialme to growl, whimper, and purr.

By then, Bill's eyes were drooping, and they were both ready for bed.

"Bill Griffin, please stay awake for another minute. Sorry if I am interrupting your revelry in there," crackled the cabin intercom. It was freaking Captain Rane. Not such a happy ending.

"Captain, how good to hear from you," he said, looking around, trying to locate the source of the sound.

"Yes, well, I would be remiss if I did not congratulate you as well as the others on a successful mission. Well done, Earthling."

He thought he heard just a touch of softness in her words but answered her professionally. "Thank you, Captain. Appreciate it."

"And I appreciate having my Ryv… having Ryval back to help us in our ultimate mission. Thank you. And thank you for bringing Yew back as well."

"Glad to know you missed me," Bill said hesitantly, although that may be pushing things a tad too far.

"Not you, Bill Griffin. Yew, our friend the wish granter, Yew."

"Whatever," Bill said as he finally understood. "Can I get some sleep now, Captain?"

"Yes, rest. We must take evasive measures for a time to make sure Blue Balzar is not on our trail. After debriefing, we shall be on our way. That is all."

Bill and Nialme found their way to the bed, Bill stumbling with fatigue and satiation. They curled around each other to sleep. Bill petted Nialme's soft fur and settled into a spooning position.

"You are the best surprise in this place and time, Nialme," he whispered. "Thank you for being a little ray of warmth and comfort in this crazy galaxy."

"I, too, am happy you are with us, Bill Griffin," she answered. "But before you sleep? May I add to your treasures of memory?"

He propped himself on an elbow and kissed her cheek. "Trust me, Nialme, you are already the best of memories."

He heard a little cracking sound, like a can of ale back home getting squeezed and crunched. She was fussing with something on her back, down near her beautiful ass. And then she brought it up to him, one of the plates from her back. She handed it to him and made herself comfortable again, snuggling up against his stomach.

"Wait, what's this? Did that hurt?"

"This is for you to have and to hold as a memory. There was no harm to me, the gift will grow back. You should not worry." She yawned and settled with a sigh. "I want you to have things, mementos of your past, Bill Griffin. But I want you to have lots of new memories, too. I want you to remember me always. No matter what."

Even if this were merely a dream, Bill could never forget this tantalizing soft creature wrapped in his arms.

-To be continued in Book 2-

If you liked the story, please take a moment to leave a review at your favorite retailer.

Here is a preview of the **next story** you may enjoy:

ZIPPING UP his suit, Bill ran into the hall, desperately sending his thoughts out to Qeet.

Hey, report in, please? I need help and company, here.

He felt, more than heard the chirrups from his little friend, and with a flash of white, Qeet suddenly appeared on Bill's shoulder. He fluffed his feathered arms and rubbed his walnut-sized eyes then nuzzled Bill's neck.

"Mr. Bill Griffin good mornin', good morning! We slept the whole night through! Good mornin' Good mornin' to YOOUUUU!"

"Oh, for God's sake, Qeet. Were you up late watching Singin' in the Rain?"

Qeet gave a sleepy lopsided smile and nodded. "Qeet loves the rain, Bill Griffin."

"Well, right now we have a bigger problem than your never getting to see a nice earthly downpour, Qeet. I think Kimra's in trouble."

"Trouble? Never trouble trouble, 'til trouble troubles you."

"Qeet! Attention, please? I just checked in with a number of crew members. Everyone's still asleep. But I couldn't find Kimra. BG says to hit the T button here," Bill said, and he went ahead and pressed the button on his right forearm, "but I wanted someone here with me in case we run into something I can't handle alone. I might need you to teleport for help."

"Help! I need somebody!"

"Qeet. Stop with the earth media. Please. I think this is serious."

"Got it, Bill Griffin. Is BG responding to your button push?"

Bill looked down at his prosthetic hand. It flashed, but in a dull throbbing kind of way, tomato red and a soft sage green. Bill made a shushing sign with his human hand as BG started communicating.

Checking stats for all crew members who have taken leave.

"Is that what 'T' was for, Qeet wonders?" Qeet leaned over to peer at Bill's buttons. "Taken?"

"Taken?" Bill said, jerking his head up. "Well, I fucking hope not. What if somebody took my, um, our, Kimra?" A surge of panic flooded him.

If you enjoyed this sample then look for **Blue Balzar - Book 2**.

About the Author: W. D. Banecroft

W. D. Banecroft was a loner in his youth, yet he was never lonely. Wild travels in fast spaceships and adventures to far away planetary systems filled his young mind.

Now he shares those adventures so that they live on in the minds of his readers.

Connect with W. D. Banecroft

I really appreciate you reading my book! Here are my social media details:

Friend me on Facebook: https://www.facebook.com/WD-Banecroft-104677791090750

Follow me on Twitter: https://twitter.com/WdBanecroft

Check me out on Goodreads: https://www.goodreads.com/book/show/51324332-blue-balzar

Subscribe to my newsletter: https://wdbanecroft.com/newsletter/

Visit my website: https://wdbanecroft.com/